There were tears on Chloe's face as she sat staring unseeingly into the darkness.

Every haunting memory of that time, seven years before, was conspiring to remind her that she had indeed been hardly more than a child just emerging into womanhood.

And I indulged myself with a child's dreams, she thought bitterly. *Ignored the warnings from people who'd known him so much longer and so much better than I had, and who, therefore, had no illusions about him.*

I was young and stupid. I let his touch, his kisses tempt me to forget what I really wanted from life. And, oh, God, he made it so easy for me. So terribly, heartbreakingly easy.

She shivered suddenly, wrapping her arms round her body.

I mustn't use emotive words like that, she told herself. *My heart did not break. Darius was just a diversion. A painful but necessary lesson.*

And I won't make the same mistake again.

All about the author...
Sara Craven

SARA CRAVEN was born in South Devon and grew up in a house full of books. She worked as a local journalist, covering everything from flower shows to murders, and started writing for Mills and Boon in 1975. When not writing, she enjoys films, music, theatre, cooking and eating in good restaurants. She now lives near her family in Warwickshire. Sara has appeared as a contestant on the former Channel Four game show *Fifteen to One,* and in 1997 was the UK television *Mastermind* champion. In 2005 she was a member of the Romantic Novelists' team on *University Challenge—the Professionals.*

Other titles by Sara Craven available in ebook:

Harlequin Presents®

2992—THE HIGHEST STAKES OF ALL
2961—HIS UNTAMED INNOCENT

Sara Craven

THE END OF HER INNOCENCE

TORONTO NEW YORK LONDON
AMSTERDAM PARIS SYDNEY HAMBURG
STOCKHOLM ATHENS TOKYO MILAN MADRID
PRAGUE WARSAW BUDAPEST AUCKLAND

Recycling programs
for this product may
not exist in your area.

ISBN-13: 978-0-373-13055-9

THE END OF HER INNOCENCE

First North American Publication 2012

www.Harlequin.com

Printed in U.S.A.

THE END OF HER INNOCENCE

CHAPTER ONE

'BUT, Chloe, I need you with us. I'm counting on you.' Mrs Armstrong opened limpid blue eyes to their widest extent. 'I thought you knew that.'

She paused. 'Besides, just think of it—an entire summer in the South of France. And we'll be away quite a lot, so you'd have the villa all to yourself. Now, isn't that tempting?'

'Yes, it is,' Chloe Benson returned equably. 'But, as I said when I handed in my notice, madam, I have my own plans.'

And staying in domestic service, no matter how gold-plated and lucrative, is not among them, she added silently. Nice try, Dilys baby, but no thanks.

'Well, I'm very disappointed.' Mrs Armstrong's tone took on the faint peevishness which was her nearest approach to animation. 'And I don't know what my husband will say.'

He'll say, 'Bad luck, old thing,' then go back to the *Financial Times*, just as he always does, Chloe thought, biting back a smile.

'If it's a question of money.' Mrs Armstrong allowed her perfect brow to wrinkle. 'If you've had a better offer, I'm sure we could come to some arrangement.'

On the contrary, Chloe wanted to tell her, it's love rather than money that's luring me away.

She allowed herself a happy moment to think about Ian. To summon up the image of his tall, broad-shouldered frame, his curling brown hair and smiling blue eyes. To imagine the moment when she'd go into his arms and say, 'I've come home, darling, and this time it's for good. Just name the day and I'll be there.'

She shook her head. 'It's nothing like that, madam. I've simply decided to take a different career direction.'

'But what a waste, when you're so good at what you do.'

What talent did you really require for saying, 'Yes, madam, very good madam?' Chloe wondered with faint exasperation. For organising the smooth running of a house with every modern convenience known to the mind of man and then some. For making sure the other members of staff did their jobs efficiently.

Whatever might be happening in the City, billionaire Hugo Armstrong wanted an untroubled existence at his country home, Colestone Manor. He was bored by day-to-day domestic detail, requiring any problems to be dealt with quickly and unobtrusively, the bills paid, and his guests offered the luxurious environment of a top hotel.

Quite simply, he asked for perfection, with the minimum effort on his part, and, during her tenure as housekeeper, Chloe had ensured that he got it.

She knew she was young for the job and she would have a lot to prove, but she was bright, energetic and a good organiser used to hard work, as her previous references attested.

Her responsibilities were manifold, her hours long, but her astonishing salary more than compensated for these and other inconveniences.

She was not, of course, expected to have any life of her own. Christmas and Easter were busy times at the Manor. She had not even been able to attend Uncle Hal and Aunt Libby's thirtieth wedding anniversary, because the Armstrongs had arranged a large house-party that weekend, and couldn't spare her. Her salary that month had been augmented by a large bonus, but it hardly made up for missing out on such a special occasion with people she loved, the only real family she'd ever had, and she still had feelings of guilt about it.

But she'd always known that the job was twenty-four-seven while it lasted. And now her notice was nearly up, and it was only going to last another week.

Losing her might cause her employers some temporary annoyance, she reflected as she went back to her quarters, but no-one was indispensable, and the Belgravia agency would supply a replacement for her with the minimum of fuss, so she was hardly leaving them in the lurch.

The computer in the housekeeper's office was regularly updated with details of the shops that delivered the Manor's supplies, and the tradesmen who provided any services required, plus the family's food preferences, fads and fancies, as well as a complete rundown on all meals served to guests over the past six months, and the bedrooms they'd occupied where appropriate.

Her successor, she thought with satisfaction, should enjoy a seamless takeover.

She would miss her flat, she admitted as she closed its door behind her and looked around. Though small, it was self-contained, and luxuriously equipped with its own wet room, an expensive fitted galley kitchen, and a queen-sized bed dominating the bedroom.

It would seem odd sleeping in the modest room at Axford Grange again, with Aunt Libby filling a hot-water bottle for her whether she needed it or not, and popping in to say goodnight, but it would not be for long.

Maybe Ian would want her to move in with him before they were married, she thought pleasurably. And if he did, she would agree without the slightest hesitation. It was more than time his patient wooing was rewarded. In fact, she couldn't understand why she'd held back for so long. At twenty-five and still a virgin, she was beginning to feel as if she was part of an endangered species.

And yet she'd remained celibate entirely through her own choice. Her creamy skin, tip-tilted hazel eyes with their long lashes and warmly curving mouth had attracted plenty of male attention since her teens.

She'd been sixteen when Ian arrived at the Grange on placement from his veterinary college and, almost from the first, she'd been sure that they were meant for each other.

As soon as he was qualified, he'd come back to work in her uncle's busy practice, and he was now a full partner.

Soon he'll be my partner too, she thought and smiled to herself.

He'd proposed for the first time just after she'd left university, but she'd demurred, knowing she wanted to test her newly fledged wings. She'd planned to work as a magazine journalist but jobs in the industry proved elusive, and as a temporary measure she'd joined an agency offering domestic help. Most of her friends at college had worked in bars or waited on restaurant tables to supplement their money, but Chloe, with Aunt Libby's training behind her, opted for cleaning jobs instead, working in the early mornings and earning a reputation for being reliable, fast and thorough.

She'd just laughed when she was nicknamed Chloe the Char, retorting 'honest work for honest pay'. Her view on that had never changed.

Ian had not been at all happy when she told him she'd been offered the job at Colestone Manor.

'It's one hell of a distance from here,' he'd protested. 'I thought you were going to find something locally. That we were going to have some real time together at last.'

'And so we shall,' she said. 'But it's also a chance to make some real money.'

'I'm not exactly earning peanuts,' he returned, his mouth tightening. 'You won't be living in penury.'

'I know.' She kissed him. 'But have you any idea what even the smallest wedding costs these days? And Uncle Hal and Aunt Libby have done so much for me all my life. This is one expense I can spare them. Besides, the time will soon pass. You'll see.'

Only it hadn't, and Chloe wondered sometimes whether she'd have taken the job if she'd realised how all-consuming it was, with the Armstrongs quite reasonably expecting her to be at their beck and call all day and every day.

Communication with Ian and the family over the past year had been largely through hurried notes and phone calls. Not a satisfactory state of affairs by any means.

But all that was behind her now, she thought, and she could concentrate on the future and turning herself into the ideal niece and the perfect fiancée.

Because of her savings, of course, she didn't even need to find another job—not immediately. So, she could take her time. Look around. Find the right thing, and stick to it for a couple of years until they decided to start a family.

It was all going to work out perfectly, she told herself and sighed with contentment.

She was waiting for the coffee percolator to finish brewing, when she heard a knock, and Tanya, the nanny to the Armstrong twins put her head round the door.

'The rumour mill is working overtime,' she announced. 'Tell me it's wrong for once, and you're not leaving after all.'

'Oh, but I am.' Chloe smiled at her and took down a second beaker.

'Tragedy.' Tanya slumped into a chair, stretching out long legs, her pretty freckled face disconsolate. 'Where can I go for sanity when the brats are driving me mad?'

'What have you done with them at the moment? Tied them to chairs in the nursery?'

'Dilys is taking them to a tea party—mummies only,' Tanya said grimly. 'I wish her luck.'

'My sympathies are with the hostess,' Chloe returned, pouring the coffee.

'Well, spare a thought for me. I'll be the one left holding the baby—literally—in the South of France while Dilys and Hugo do the Grand Tour from villa to villa and yacht to yacht,' Tanya said moodily. 'The only thing holding me together was the prospect of you being there too. I was sure she'd persuade you. Get you to withdraw your notice.'

'She certainly tried,' Chloe said cheerfully, handing her a beaker. 'But no dice. I'm off to get a life.'

'You have a new job lined up?'

'Not as such.' Chloe hesitated. 'Actually, I'm going to be married.'

Tanya's eyes went to her bare left hand. 'To that vet you mentioned back home? I didn't know you were even engaged.'

'Well, it's strictly unofficial as yet. I wasn't ready before when he asked me, but, now, settling down seems like a really great thing to do, so,' she added, smiling, 'I'm going to do it.'

'Won't village life seem tame after all this glitz and glamour?'

Chloe shook her head. 'I've never bought into it, any more than you have. I know my priorities and this job was always just a means to an end.

'Apart from getting my hair cut once a month,' she went on, running a hand through her mop of dark curls. 'And having the odd cinema and pizza jaunt with you when we could get time off together, I've hardly spent a thing. So I have a lot of money sitting in the bank right now.'

Her smile widened. 'Enough to pay for a wedding, certainly, and also contribute to the updating of Ian's cottage, which it sorely needs. Together, we can make it wonderful.'

Tanya's brows lifted. 'Does Ian share this view?'

Chloe sighed humorously. 'He seems to think all a kitchen requires is a stove, a sink and a second-hand fridge. Also that a rusting bath is a valuable antique. I intend to educate him.'

'Well, good luck to that.' Tanya raised her beaker in a faintly ironic toast. 'But maybe he's already put in a new kitchen in honour of your return. Did you think of that?'

'He doesn't yet know I'm coming back. I want to surprise him.'

'Christmas!' Tanya eyed her quizzically. 'You must be very sure of him.'

'I'm sure of us both,' Chloe told her serenely. 'And I can't wait to get back to Willowford.' She sighed again. 'I've missed it so much.'

'It must be a hell of a place to coax you away from the Riviera,' Tanya commented. 'What's so special about it?'

'Well, it's not exactly picture-postcard stuff,' Chloe said, frowning. 'There are no thatched roofs, and the church is Victorian. Although the Hall is considered rather splendid—Jacobean with later additions.'

'And does it have a squire who twirls his moustaches and chases the village maidens?'

Chloe's smile held faint constraint. 'I don't think that's Sir Gregory's style,' she said, after a pause. 'Even if his arthritis allowed it.'

'Is he married?'

Chloe shook her head. 'A widower.'

'Children?'

'Two sons.'

'The heir and the spare,' said Tanya. 'Very conventional.'

Chloe bit her lip. 'Not really, because the spare doesn't

feature much any more. There was a gigantic rift a few years ago, and he became *persona non grata*.'

'Aha.' Tanya's eyes gleamed. 'This is more like it. What happened?'

Chloe looked away. 'He had an affair with his older brother's wife,' she said at last. 'Broke up the marriage. All very sordid and nasty. So his father threw him out.'

'What happened to the wife?'

'She left too.'

'So are they together? She and—what do they call him?—I can't go on saying "the spare".'

'Darius,' Chloe said. 'Darius Maynard. And I don't think anyone knows where he is or what happened to him. Or even cares, for that matter.'

Tanya drew a deep breath. 'Well the place is clearly a seething mass of steaming passion and illicit desire. I can see why you want to get in on the action. And the heir needs another wife, presumably.' She gave a wicked wink. 'Maybe you could do better than a country vet.'

'No way.' Chloe drained her beaker. 'To be honest, I think quite a few people found Andrew Maynard a bit of a stuffed shirt and didn't altogether blame Penny, who was incredibly beautiful, for looking around. But Darius already had a bad name locally, so no-one ever thought he'd be the one to get a second glance.'

Tanya's eyes gleamed. 'What sort of bad name?'

'Expelled from school. Drinking, gambling, mixing with the local wild bunch. Parties that people only whispered about behind their hands.' Chloe shrugged. 'Plus rumours that he was involved in other even worse things—illegal dog fighting, for instance.' She added bleakly, 'No-one was sorry to see him go, believe me.'

'Well, for all that, he sounds more interesting than his brother.' Tanya finished her coffee and stood up. 'I'd better get back. I thought while the monsters were missing, I could fumigate the toy cupboards.'

Left alone, Chloe washed out the beakers and put them in the drying rack.

For the life of her, she could not fathom why she'd told Tanya all that stuff about the Maynard family. It was seven years since it had happened, she thought, and should have been relegated long ago to some mental dump bin.

She suddenly had an image of a man's face, tanned and arrogant, nose and cheekbones strongly, almost harshly, sculpted, the mouth wide and sensual. From beneath a swathe of dirty-blond hair, compelling green eyes had stared at the world with disdain, as if daring it to judge him.

Yet it had done so, and, starting with his father, had condemned him as guilty. The adulterer who'd betrayed his brother and been sentenced to exile as a result. Although that could have been no real hardship for Darius Maynard, she thought. He'd always been restless and edgy. Willowford was far too small and tame a world for him and always had been.

But it suits me just fine, she told herself, biting her lip. It's a decent little place with good people. Somewhere to put down roots and raise the next generation. It gave me a loving home when I was a small baby, and now it's given me Ian. It's security.

Sir Gregory had been part of that, she thought. A large, rather forbidding man, but rock-solid like his house. A pillar of his community, as the saying was. And Andrew Maynard was much the same. An outdoor man with a passion for climbing, more conventionally handsome than his younger brother, courteous and faintly aloof. Part of a continuing line or so it had seemed.

Except, 'Thank heaven there are no children to be hurt,' Aunt Libby had said quietly when the scandal broke.

But Darius had always been different—the joker in the pack. A throwback to some other, wilder time with his dangerous mocking smile, and cool smoky drawl.

My God—little Chloe grown up at last. Who'd have thought it?

She was suddenly aware she was gripping the edge of the sink so hard that her fingers were hurting, and released it hastily with a little gasp.

Memories were risky things, rather like pushing a stick to the bottom of a tranquil pool and watching the mud and debris rise. Far better, she thought, to let the water remain still and unsullied in case it never truly cleared again.

Oh, get a grip, she told herself impatiently as she returned to the sitting room. *Put your microscope away.*

It had all happened long ago, and should remain in the past where it belonged. If not forgotten, then ignored, as if Sir Gregory had only ever had one son. And as if that son had never married the Honourable Penelope Hatton and brought her back to Willowford Hall to tempt and be disastrously tempted in her turn.

I thought she was the most beautiful thing I'd ever seen, thought Chloe. *We all did. I think I even envied her.*

But now everything's changed. I'm the one looking forward to a happy future with the man I love. And, if she knew, she might well be the one envying me.

It had been raining first thing when she set off from Colestone, but now the skies seemed to be clearing and a watery sun was showing its face.

A good omen, Chloe thought happily, switching the car radio to a music station, and humming along as she drove.

Rather to her surprise, she'd found herself genuinely sorry to leave the Manor. After all, she mused, it had been the focus of her attention for the past year. Besides, however indolent and self-absorbed they might be, the Armstrongs had been generous employers in the only way they knew, and she'd liked the other staff.

In the bag beside her on the passenger seat was the pretty carriage clock they'd bought her as a farewell present, and she'd been moved almost to tears as she thanked them and promised it pride of place on her future mantelpiece.

'As for you,' she'd muttered as she hugged Tanya. 'I'm going to be needing a bridesmaid.'

'Happy to oblige,' Tanya whispered back. 'Unless I get arrested for twin-strangling in the meantime.'

Her successor had arrived—a widow in her forties with a brisk air. She had dismissed Chloe's computer system, saying that she had her own methods, at the same time running a suspicious finger along the office windowsill in search of non-existent dust.

Life at the Manor, Chloe thought wryly as she wished her luck, could become quite interesting quite soon.

She stopped at a roadside pub for a lunch of ham sandwiches and coffee to fuel her for the final two hours of her journey, choosing a table outside in a sheltered corner of the garden where bees were busy among the honeysuckle.

With the excitement of all the coming reunions bubbling away inside her, she almost had to force herself to eat.

As she poured her second cup of coffee, she reached into her bag for her mobile phone.

She'd called Aunt Libby again the previous evening to tell her what time she hoped to arrive, and while her aunt had seemed her usual warm self, Chloe had detected another faint nuance beneath the welcoming words.

'Is something wrong?' she'd asked at last. Libby Jackson had hesitated.

'I was wondering if you'd spoken to Ian yet—informed him you were coming home, this time for good.'

'But I told you, Aunt Libby, I want to surprise him.'

'Yes, darling, so you said.' Another pause. 'But I can't help thinking that a complete change of your whole life-plan like this, which involves him so closely, really needs some prior warning.'

'Not unless he's developed some serious heart condition and you think the shock could kill him.' Chloe was amused. 'Is that it?'

'God forbid,' said her aunt. 'When last seen, he looked as strong as a horse. But I keep thinking of these dreadful surprise parties people keep giving, which I'm sure are far more fun for the organisers than the recipients. Just a thought, my dear.'

And maybe it was a good one, Chloe decided, clicking on Ian's number. But it went straight to voicemail, indicating that he was working. So she left a message then rang the cottage, and announced herself on the answer-phone too.

Belt and braces, Aunt Libby, she thought. So now he should be ready and waiting.

She smiled to herself as she replaced the phone, imagining the smile in his eyes when he saw her, the warmth of his arms around her, and the touch of his lips on hers.

He was so worth waiting for, she thought gratefully. And now she was back, she would not leave again.

She had five miles still to go when the petrol warning light suddenly appeared on the dashboard, when only fifteen minutes before it had been registering half-full.

Chloe wrinkled her nose, wondering which was the true reading. 'Memo to self,' she murmured. 'Take the car to Tom Sawley's garage and get the gauge seen to. Particularly before the MOT becomes due again.'

Fortunately, she was approaching a turning for the main road, where there was a small filling station only a few hundred yards away.

All three pumps were busy when she arrived, so she joined the shortest queue, and got out of the car stretching.

And then she saw it, parked over by the wall, its number plate as familiar to her as that of her own car.

Ian's jeep, she thought joyously. What was more, the bonnet was up, and there he was bending over the engine with his back to her, his long legs encased in blue denim, as he made some adjustment.

She was sure he would sense her presence and turn, but he was leaning too far over, intent on what he was doing.

As soon as she was within touching distance, she reached for him, her mouth curving mischievously as she ran her fingers over the taut male buttocks and slid one hand between his thighs.

He yelped and sprang upright, cursing as he hit his head on the bonnet.

And as he did so, Chloe backed away gasping, praying for the ground to open up beneath her.

But it remained heartlessly intact, so that she was still there, open-mouthed with horror when the man swung round, and looked at her, his blond hair tousled, and the green eyes blazing.

'What the bloody hell do you think you're playing at?' asked Darius Maynard, his voice a snarl of pure anger. 'Or have you just gone raving mad?'

CHAPTER TWO

CHLOE took another step backwards, aware that she was burning from the soles of her feet up to her hairline, and probably beyond.

Oh, God, let me wake up, she prayed frantically, and find this is only a nightmare.

When she could speak, she said hoarsely, 'You—*you!* What are you doing with Ian's jeep?'

'Correction,' he said brusquely. 'My jeep for the past eight weeks. Cartwright was trading it in for a newer model and I bought it.'

'You've been back here for two months?'

'For over six, actually.' He added curtly, 'If it's any concern of yours, Miss Benson.'

Her flush deepened, if that was possible. 'I—I didn't realise.'

What on earth was going on? she wondered. Why had he returned when his banishment was supposed to have been permanent? How could that kind of breach possibly have been healed? Sir Gregory surely wasn't the type to welcome back the prodigal son. And how did Andrew, the betrayed husband, feel about it?

Above all, why had no-one mentioned it? How was it Ian hadn't said, 'By the way, I've sold my jeep, and to Darius Maynard of all people.'

'Why would you know?' He hunched an indifferent shoulder. 'You haven't been around much to catch up on the local sensations.'

'I've been working.'

'Most people do,' he said. 'Or are you claiming particular credit?'

I am not going to do this, Chloe told herself, swallowing back the impetuous retort that had risen to her lips. I am not going to stand here bandying jibes with Darius Maynard.

Because he's perfectly correct. However I may feel about it, his return is absolutely none of my business and I must remember that. I will remember it.

'Not at all.' She glanced at her watch. 'And now I must be going.' She took a deep breath. 'I—apologise for what just happened. It was a genuine mistake.'

'It must have been,' he drawled. 'After all, we were never exactly on goosing terms, were we, Miss Benson? I wasn't aware you had that kind of relationship with Cartwright either.'

'Clearly, you also have some catching up to do.' She turned away. 'Goodbye, Mr Maynard.'

She got back in her car, started the engine and swung the vehicle out of the forecourt towards the Willowford Road.

I'm shaking like a leaf, she thought, which is totally ridiculous. Yes, I've just made a complete fool of myself, but if it had been anyone else, they'd probably have helped me to laugh off the embarrassment somehow, not made it worse.

Of all the people in the world I never wanted to see again, he must be in pole position. Yet here he is, turning up like the proverbial bad penny. I wish I could ignore him, but we both have to live in the same small community, so that's impossible.

On the other hand, she thought, his return might be purely temporary. He'd frequently been absent in the old days, and might not be planning to stay for any length of time now. That was what she would hope for, anyway.

Besides, she added firmly, she would be too busy planning her wedding and her life with Ian to pay any heed to the Hall, and the vagaries of its occupants.

She'd travelled about a mile when the petrol light showed it meant business by letting the car slide slowly but very definitely to a halt.

Swearing under her breath, Chloe steered it to the verge. She'd had one thing on her mind at the filling station—escape—and this, of course, was what it had led to. Something else she could lay firmly at Darius Maynard's damned door, she thought, fuming.

She could use her mobile, she supposed. Send out an SOS to Uncle Hal or Ian to come to her rescue, but that, apart from leaving her looking like an idiot twice in one day, wasn't exactly the upbeat, triumphant return to Willowford that she had planned.

Better, she thought, grimacing, to start hiking, and as she reached for the door handle, she saw in her mirror the jeep come round the corner, drive past her, then pull in a few yards ahead.

She felt a silent scream rise in her throat, as Darius Maynard got out and walked back to her.

No, no, *no*! she wailed inwardly. This couldn't be happening. It wasn't possible.

'Having problems?'

'Absolutely not,' she said. 'Just—collecting my thoughts.'

'Pity you didn't collect some petrol while you were about it,' he commented caustically. 'I presume that was your purpose in the filling station, rather than renewing our acquaintance in that unique manner. And that's why you're stuck here?'

'Whatever,' Chloe returned curtly, loathing him. 'But I can cope.'

'Presumably by drilling for oil in the adjoining field. However, God forbid I should leave a damsel in distress.'

'Especially when you cause most of it.' She made her voice poisonously sweet, and he winced elaborately.

'Giving a dog a bad name, Miss Benson? Inappropriate behaviour, I'd have thought, for someone with her eye on a vet.'

She bit her lip. 'It happens that Ian Cartwright and I are engaged.'

'Good God,' he said. 'Does he know that?'

'What the hell do you mean?' Chloe demanded furiously. 'We're engaged and we'll be married by the end of the summer.'

'You know best,' he said softly. 'But I do hope you're not mistaking a girlhood crush for the real thing, Miss Benson. You're no longer a susceptible teenager, you know.'

She said in a small choked voice, 'How dare you? How bloody dare you? Just get out of here and leave me in peace.'

'Not without lending a kindly hand to a neighbour,' Damian retorted, apparently unperturbed. 'The jeep is diesel as I'm sure you remember, but I do have a petrol can in the back, and a brisk walk back to the filling station in the sunshine should do wonders for your temper.'

He paused. 'So, do you want it, or would you prefer to wait for the next chivalrous passer-by, yes or no?'

She would have actually preferred to see him wearing his rotten can, jammed down hard, but she bit her lip and nodded. 'Thank you.'

'Boy, that must have hurt.' His grin mocked her, before he turned and strode back to the jeep, lean-hipped and lithe.

He hadn't changed, she thought with sudden bewilderment, watching him go. The past seven years didn't seem to have touched him at all. Yet how was that possible?

No conscience, she thought bitterly. No regret for the havoc he'd caused. The ruined lives he'd left behind him.

She picked up her jacket from the passenger seat, and let herself out of the car. As she unfastened the boot, Darius came back with the can. He glanced down at the array of luggage and whistled.

'My God, Willowford's own Homecoming Queen. You really do mean to stay, don't you?'

'Yes.' She placed her jacket carefully across the top-most case, smoothing its folds as she did so. Hiding, she realised with annoyance, the fact that her hands were shaking. 'I have every reason to do so.'

'But I don't.' His mouth was smiling but his eyes were hard as glass. 'Is that the hidden message you're trying to convey?'

'As you said, it's none of my concern.' She held out her hand for the can. 'I'll make sure this is returned to you.'

'By courier, no doubt.' He shrugged. 'Forget it. I have others. And now, I fear, I must tear myself away.' He walked towards the jeep, then turned.

'I wish you a joyful reunion with your family and friends, Miss Benson,' he said softly. 'But as for that peace you mentioned—I wouldn't count on it, because you're not the peaceful kind. Not in your heart. You just haven't realised it yet.'

He swung himself into the jeep and drove off, leaving her staring after him, her heart pounding uncomfortably.

'You've lost weight,' said Aunt Libby.

'That is so not true.' Chloe hugged her again. 'I'm the same to the ounce as I was a year ago. I swear it.'

She looked round the big comfortable kitchen with its Aga, big pine table and tall Welsh dresser holding her aunt's prized collection of blue-and-white china and sighed rapturously. 'Gosh, it's wonderful to be home.'

'No-one forced you to go away,' said Aunt Libby, lifting the kettle from the Aga and filling the teapot. Her tone was teasing, but her swift glance was serious.

Chloe shrugged. 'They made me an offer I couldn't refuse. You know that. Besides it's been an education, seeing how the other half live.'

'The village will seem very dull after Millionaires Row.'

'On the contrary, I know for sure where I belong.' Chloe paused. 'Has Ian called? I took your advice and rang him to say I was arriving.'

'I think he was out at Farsleigh today. It's a bad reception area.' Her aunt passed her a plate of raisin bread.

'Heaven,' said Chloe, as she took a slice, smiling to conceal her disappointment over Ian. 'Is this the Jackson equivalent of the fatted calf—to welcome home the prodigal?' And paused again, taking a deep breath. 'So, how is everything and—everyone?' She tried to sound casual. 'Any major changes anywhere?'

'Nothing much.' Mrs Jackson poured the tea. 'I gather Sir Gregory is making progress at last, poor man.' She sighed. 'What a tragedy that was. I'm not a superstitious woman, but it's almost as if there's been some dreadful curse on the Maynard family.'

Chloe stared at her, the flippant retort that there was and that she'd seen it alive and well an hour ago dying on her lips.

'What do you mean?'

Mrs Jackson looked surprised. 'Well, I was thinking of Andrew, of course, being killed in that dreadful accident.'

Chloe's cup clattered back into its saucer. 'Andrew Maynard—dead?' She stared at her aunt. 'Never!'

'Why, yes, dear. Surely you saw it in the papers? And I told you about it in one of my letters.'

Had she? Chloe wondered guiltily, knowing that, once she'd made sure that everyone at Axford Grange was well and happy, she hadn't always read on to the end.

'I—I must have missed a page somewhere. What happened?'

'He was in the Cairngorms climbing alone as he often did. Apparently, there was a rock fall, and he was swept away.' She shuddered. 'Horrible.'

'And Sir Gregory?'

Aunt Libby shook her head. 'A stroke, brought on by the news.'

Chloe picked up her cup. Swallowed some tea. Schooled her voice to normality. 'I thought I glimpsed Darius Maynard when I stopped for petrol. Is that why he's come back? Because he's now the heir?'

'I think that it was concern for his father rather than the inheritance that brought him.' Aunt Libby spoke with gentle reproof and Chloe flushed.

'Of course. I'm sorry. It's just that I've—never liked him.'

'Something for which your uncle and I were always profoundly grateful,' her aunt said with a touch of grimness. 'He was always far too attractive for his own good.' She sighed again. 'But he's certainly provided Sir Gregory with the very best of care, hiring a charming girl as his live-in nurse who seems to have inspired the poor man and literally brought him back from the grave.

'And Mr Crosby, the agent, reckons Darius is really putting his back into running the estate these days, so perhaps he's become a reformed character during his absence.'

And maybe pigs might fly, thought Chloe. She took another piece of raisin bread. 'And—Mrs Maynard. Penny. Is he still with her?'

'No-one knows or dare ask. She's certainly not at the Hall. And she didn't attend Andrew's funeral, or the memorial service.' Mrs Jackson refilled her niece's cup. 'Apparently Mrs Thursgood at the post office asked Darius straight out if he was married—well, she would!—and he just laughed, and said, "God, no". So we're none the wiser.'

'But it's hardly a surprise,' Chloe said evenly. 'He's never been the marrying kind.'

'On the other hand, he's never been the next baronet before either,' Aunt Libby pointed out, cutting into a handsome Victoria sponge. 'That may change things.'

'Perhaps so.' Chloe shrugged. 'Maybe he's considering the charming nurse up at the Hall.'

'Lindsay?' Her aunt sounded almost startled. 'Oh, I don't think she'd do for him at all.'

'But, then, who would?' Chloe helped herself to a piece of sponge with its strawberry jam and cream filling. 'If I go on like this,' she added wryly, 'I'll be the size of a house by the time of the wedding.'

Aunt Libby gave her a swift glance, then looked back at her plate. 'Nonsense,' she said firmly. 'If anything, you could do with a few pounds. Real men don't want skeletons to cuddle.'

The wisdom according to Uncle Hal, no doubt, Chloe thought with an inward smile.

They were such darlings. Living proof of how well marriage could work, given the chance. And if their childlessness had been a sadness, they'd kept it well-hidden, opening their home and their hearts to her instead, when her mother, Aunt Libby's younger sister, had died suddenly of a thrombosis only two days after giving birth.

Her father, an engineer in the oil industry had been on his way back from Saudi Arabia to see his wife and child when the tragedy happened. Devastated by his loss, and with two years of his contract still to run, he knew that taking his newborn daughter back with him was impossible. Apart from the environmental problems, he'd been an only son and had no experience with infants. He'd been almost at his wits' end when his grieving sister-in-law had stepped in, making her momentous offer, which he'd thankfully accepted.

The original plan had been that Chloe should go to him as soon as he found a more appropriate job, but another contract succeeded the first, and from the conversations the Jacksons had with him when he was in the UK on leave, they knew that he'd become an ex-pat in spirit as well as fact. That he liked his life just the way it was. And contributing to his daughter's support was as far as he was prepared to go.

Eventually they heard that he'd met an American girl and was going to remarry, and resigned themselves once more to Chloe's loss. Only it didn't happen.

Her father's new bride-to-be, Mary Theresa, had reacted badly to the idea of a female stepchild when it had been put to her, and Chloe remained in Willowford.

She'd eventually been invited to Florida to see her father and meet her stepmother, together with the twin boys born a year after the marriage, but the visit was not a success, and had not been repeated. Now he was little more than a name on a Christmas card. Her birthday was clearly a date with associations he preferred to forget, and although this was bound to sadden her, she decided she could not altogether blame him.

But at some point she would also have to decide whether he, or Uncle Hal who'd loved her like his own, should give her away at her wedding. And that could be tricky.

When tea was finished she loaded the china and cutlery into the dishwasher and switched it on, then checked her mobile phone for a message or a text from Ian, but there was nothing.

She sighed inwardly. 'Do you need a hand with supper, or shall I take my things up to my room now?' she asked her aunt, replacing the phone in her bag.

'Yes, go and unpack, dear.' There was an awkward note in Mrs Jackson's voice. 'We've been decorating upstairs, doing some renovations too, so you'll find it all rather different. I hope you don't mind.'

'On the contrary, I'm intrigued.' Chloe spoke lightly, but when she opened her bedroom door, her reaction was stunned.

It was completely unrecognisable from the cosy, slightly worn haven that she'd loved, she thought numbly.

The rose-coloured carpet she'd begged for in her early teens had vanished, replaced by stripped, sanded and varnished boards. The pretty sprigged wallpaper had given away to plain walls in a rich, deep cream, and the curtains she'd made herself to go with the carpet had disappeared too. The new drapes were in a vivid blue, matching the tailored spread fitting the single brass bed.

The familiar shabby furniture had gone, but the small cast-iron fireplace was still there, filled with a display of blue teasels. And a fitted cream wardrobe and a mirrored dressing chest now occupied the alcoves on either side of the chimney breast, which Uncle Hal had once shelved to hold her books, toys and ornaments.

It was smart, shiny and new, and it looked terrific, but it was now very much a guest room, she realised with a swift pang. There was nothing left of her at all.

And the bathroom across the passage was an equal shock. The big cast-iron bath and wide basin had made way for a modern white suite, glittering with chrome accessories, and a glass cubicle with a power shower had been installed in the remaining space, while the walls and floor were tiled in turquoise and white.

But what's brought all this on? Have they had a lottery win I don't know about? Chloe wondered as she went back to the room that no longer belonged to her. Although the window seat was still there, and the view over open fields where cows grazed quietly hadn't changed.

She paused, her mouth twisting. Oh, for heaven's sake, she thought with sudden impatience. You're a grown woman, not a child to be hankering for a pink carpet, a collection of pottery owls and a complete set of the *Famous Five* books.

Things change, and you're about to move on yourself, so stop whingeing and get a grip.

She unpacked swiftly and neatly, stowed her cases under the bed, then returned downstairs.

Aunt Libby turned from the Aga with a look of faint apprehension as she entered the kitchen.

'What happened? Did some TV makeover team come knocking at the door? It all looks amazing.' Chloe knew her smile was a little too wide and too bright, but her aunt seemed reassured.

'Well, no, darling. Your uncle and I have a different reason for smartening the place up.' She paused. 'You see, we've decided to downsize.'

'Downsize?' Chloe's smile was wiped away, and replaced by shock. 'You mean you're—going to sell the Grange?' A thought struck her. 'Oh, heavens, has something happened to the practice? Is it the recession?'

'No, no, on the contrary.' Mrs Jackson's reassurance was swift. 'It's busier than ever, and that's the problem. It's always been a twenty-four-hour service, and your uncle isn't getting any younger.

'It's been a wonderful life, of course, and he's never wanted anything different, but now he's seriously considering retirement. Giving himself time to do the things he's never been able to fully enjoy before. His fishing, for instance. And he might even take up golf again. And we both used to love quite serious walking.

'So, they've been interviewing for a new assistant, and one

of Ian's friends from college might be interested in becoming a partner.'

'This isn't just a dream for the future, is it?' Chloe said slowly. 'This is a real plan for now.'

'Well, nothing will happen for a while, and wherever we go, there'll always be a place for you, Chloe. Never doubt that. But, at the same time, we know you have your own life to lead and we're so proud and so happy for you.'

'But you're not intending to leave the area, surely?' Chloe felt as if the flagged floor was shifting under her feet.

'Almost certainly,' her aunt said briskly.

'But I thought you loved Willowford.'

'It's a fine place,' Mrs Jackson nodded. 'And it's been good to us, but I don't think your uncle and I ever felt we'd end our days here. We've had a survey and valuation done on the Grange, and it seems we can afford to pick and choose where we'll go next.' She smiled. 'It's quite an adventure.'

'Yes,' Chloe agreed quietly. 'Indeed it is.'

And I—I have my own adventure to embark on too, so I shouldn't begrudge Uncle and Auntie a thing.

'We've started de-cluttering, as they call it, already,' Aunt Libby went on. 'You gather so much stuff over the years that you don't need, so the charity shops for miles around have reaped the benefit.

'Oh, not your things, darling,' she added quickly. 'We boxed and labelled it all for you, and put the cartons up in the attic, ready for whenever you want them.'

There'd be room at the cottage for them, thought Chloe. Although she'd get rid of the toys, except for the teddy bear her father had bought on his way home from Saudi to see his wife and new daughter. And the books which she'd keep for her own children—when they came along.

She waited for the usual glow of anticipation that occurred whenever she contemplated her future with Ian, but, for once, it seemed curiously muted. On the other hand, her entire homecoming hadn't been as expected either. It had been thrown off course by that dire humiliation at the filling station and had never really recovered.

I'll be better when I hear from Ian, she told herself, and at that same moment the telephone rang in the hall.

'And that's almost certainly for you,' said Aunt Libby, turning back to the meat she was browning for a cottage pie.

'So what's happened to the dream job?' Ian asked, once the 'it's wonderful to talk to you' preliminaries had been dealt with. 'Did you get fired?'

'No, of course not.' Chloe was taken aback. 'On the contrary. They wanted me to go with them for the summer to run their villa in the South of France.'

'And you turned that down for Willowford? Amazing.'

No, Chloe wanted to say. *I turned it down for you.*

Aloud, she said, 'I felt it was time to come home, back to real life again.' She paused. 'So, what time shall I see you tonight?'

He sighed. 'Can't manage tonight, Clo. There's a pony club committee meeting and I'm chairing it because Mrs Hammond's away. You must have known for ages that you'd be back today. I wish you'd told me sooner.'

'So do I.' She felt deflated, and oddly close to tears. 'But I wanted to surprise you.'

'Well you've done that all right.' He paused. 'Look, why don't I book a table at the Willowford Arms for tomorrow evening? Catch up with everything over dinner?'

Or why don't you suggest we see each other for a drink when your meeting is over? Or rush over here now?

She put a smile in her voice. 'Sounds great.'

'Then I'll pick you up just before eight,' he said briskly.

'Got to dash. I'm expecting a call from the Crawfords. Their whippet is about to litter and they're a bit concerned.'

It's a twenty-four-hour service, Chloe told herself as she put the phone down. Aunt Libby reminded you of that just now. And you've always known it—lived with it for the greater part of your life. Planned to stick with it. So you can't jib now.

A vet is like being a doctor, only the patients can't tell you their symptoms, and a successful practice is built on trust and availability. Haven't you heard Uncle Hal say so a hundred times over spoiled meals and cancelled outings?

It's not the end of the world. You've just endured one of those days, that's all, but everything starts again tomorrow.

Just keep thinking of that, and it will all work out just fine.

CHAPTER THREE

CHLOE lay back in the bath, appreciatively absorbing the scent of the rose geranium oil rising from the warm water.

In less than two hours, she'd be with Ian, and the time between would be spent pampering herself as never before.

I want to be irresistible, she thought, smiling inwardly.

All the same, she wasn't finding it as easy to slip back into the swim of things as she'd expected, although her uncle's affectionate greeting the previous evening had been balm to the soul, and he and Aunt Libby had tranquilly accepted that Ian was needed elsewhere, so she'd be eating cottage pie with them.

'That whippet's a beauty but she could be tricky. Let's hope this litter is the first and last,' had been Mr Jackson's only comment.

'So what are you doing with yourself today?' he'd asked that morning as he stood up from the breakfast table, stuffing his folded newspaper into his jacket pocket.

'Just pottering, I suppose.' Chloe had smiled at him.

'Well you could always potter over to Lizbeth Crane's, if you felt inclined,' her uncle said briskly. 'She's damaged her wrist gardening and Jack's in Brussels, so their retriever will need walking.'

'Of course I'll go.' Chloe didn't think twice. 'A wander

across the fields with a friendly dog like Flare is just what I need. I'll call round as soon as I've been to the post office.'

Which in itself had been an experience, she thought.

'So you're back.' Mrs Thursgood had greeted her with a faint sniff. 'Thought you'd deserted us for good. Come back for that young vet, I dare say. We all thought round here that the banns would have been called a year back or more. You don't want to leave it too long, missy,' she added with a look of faint disparagement. 'You're not getting any younger, and men go off the boil as quick as they go on it.'

Chloe, acutely aware that every word was being savoured by the queue behind her, paid for her stamps with murder in her heart and escaped.

But there had been more to come. She had to run the gauntlet of the shoppers in the main street, and by the time she reached the Cranes' house, she felt if one more person said, 'Well, Chloe, you're quite a stranger,' she would howl at the sky.

But Mrs Crane's delighted welcome, accompanied as it was by coffee and home-made biscuits, plus Flare's grin and gently offered paw had compensated for a great deal.

Except...

It had been a marvellous walk, the sun warm on her back, and Flare, plumy tail waving, bounding along ahead of her. After a mild disagreement over the retriever's wish to complete the pleasure of the morning by rolling joyously in a large cowpat, they turned for home. They'd just emerged from a field onto the lane leading back to the village and Chloe was fastening the gate behind her, when she heard the sound of a horse's hooves.

She glanced round and saw a handsome bay gelding trotting towards them, and paused, her throat tightening when she saw who was riding him.

'Good morning.' Darius brought the horse to a stand, and

bent forward to pat his glossy neck. 'Enjoying a constitutional, Miss Benson? I thought you'd be getting your exercise elsewhere on this lovely day—in some convenient haystack with your intended, perhaps.'

Her skin warmed. 'Do you have to make unpleasant remarks?' she asked coldly.

'On the contrary, the activity I'm referring to is entirely pleasurable.' He grinned down at her. 'Or perhaps you don't find it so. What a terrible shame, not to mention waste,' he added, his gaze sliding appreciatively over the thrust of her breasts under her white shirt, down to her slender waist and the curve of her hips.

Aware that her flush was deepening, Chloe bent hurriedly to clip on Flare's leash.

'Just as a matter of interest,' he went on. 'Why are you walking Lizbeth Crane's dog?'

'I'm being a good neighbour,' she said shortly. 'A concept you may find unfamiliar.'

'Not at all, as I hope to demonstrate over the coming months.' He paused. 'However, if true love has worked some miracle and you're really in Good Samaritan mode, you might consider extending your range as far as the Hall.'

As Chloe's lips parted to deliver a stinging refusal, he held up a hand.

'Hear me out, please. I don't get the chance to take Orion here out as much as I should, largely because any spare time I have goes to my brother's Samson, who's eating his head off in between throwing serious moodies.

'I seem to recall you were a damned good rider in the old days, so, if you'd consider exercising Orion for me sometimes, I'd be immensely grateful to you.'

She gave him a startled look. Gratitude wasn't something she'd ever have attributed to him. Or the paying of compliments. Not that it made any real difference. *I seem to recall*...

'I'm sorry,' she said. 'But it's quite impossible.'

'May I ask why?'

'I have a wedding to organise,' she said curtly. 'In case you've forgotten. I shall be far too busy.'

He sat, one hand resting on his hip, his gaze meditative as he watched her. 'I hadn't forgotten. But is it really going to take all day of every day? How many hundreds of people are you planning to invite, for God's sake?'

'That's none of your business,' she returned. 'Anyway, Arthur must still be at the Hall, so why can't he ride Orion?'

'Unfortunately, his arthritis won't let him, but it would break his heart if I pensioned him off and got a younger groom.'

He added flatly, 'And, for obvious reasons, my father finds even minor changes distressing.'

Chloe bit her lip. 'Yes—yes, of course.' She paused. 'I was—very sorry to hear about Andrew. I hadn't realised...' She took a breath. 'It was terribly sad.'

His face hardened. 'Not just sad but bloody stupid and totally unnecessary.'

She gasped. 'You don't feel, perhaps, that's too harsh a judgment? Whatever may have happened, he was still your brother.'

'Harsh, perhaps,' Darius returned coolly. 'Yet entirely accurate. However, this is not the time to debate Andrew's motives for risking his life by pushing himself to ridiculous and dangerous limits.

'And my proposition over Orion still stands,' he added. 'I'd like you to think it over, instead of just dismissing it out of hand because I'm doing the asking. You don't even have to give me a personal reply. Just ring the Hall at any time, and Arthur will have him tacked up and ready for you.'

He smiled faintly. 'And Orion would be grateful too, don't forget.'

He touched the horse with his heels, and they moved off.

Chloe stared after them, her mind a welter of mixed emotions. It was still impossible, of course—what he'd asked—but Orion was an absolute beauty, and the thought of cantering him along those flat stretches by the river in the Willow valley was a genuine temptation.

But one she had to resist.

She'd told herself the same thing at intervals during the day, and she was still saying it now as she stepped out of the bath and dried herself, and applied some of the body lotion from the satin-lined gift basket of Hermes' *Caleche* that the Armstrongs had given her for Christmas.

She repeated it as she put on her prettiest lace briefs and sprayed her arms and breasts lightly with matching scent. As she applied her make-up and combed her hair into glossy waves around her face. And as she finally slipped on the knee-skimming cream georgette dress with the deep-V neckline, which discreetly signalled that she was wearing no bra.

Too obvious? she worried in front of the mirror. Or simply a means to an end? A message to Ian that at last she was his for the taking.

Absurd to feel even remotely jittery about something that was so natural and would be so right, she thought sliding her feet into low-heeled sandals that echoed the colour of the lapis lazuli drops in her ears. Yet for some reason, she did.

Ian was in the sitting room talking to her aunt and uncle when she arrived downstairs. When he turned in response to her quiet, 'Good evening,' and saw her standing in the doorway, his jaw dropped.

'God, Clo, you look amazing—like someone from a magazine cover.'

'You look pretty good yourself.' And it wasn't just his looks, she thought as she went to him smiling, appraising his black-and-white houndstooth tweed jacket, worn with dark trousers and the ruby silk tie which set off his crisp white shirt. He'd dressed to kill too, for this important night in their lives.

It's going to be all right, she thought. It's going to be wonderful.

She lifted her face, offering him her lips, but he reddened slightly and deposited a kiss on her cheek instead.

'Have a wonderful time,' Aunt Libby whispered with a hug, as Ian paused to have a final word with Uncle Hal on their way out. 'I won't wait up.'

Chloe detected a hint of apprehension in her smile and hugged her back. 'Don't worry. I'm a big girl now. I know what I'm doing.'

When Chloe was growing up, the Willowford Arms had been just a village pub offering good beer, a dartboard and a skittle alley.

Over the years, under successive landlords, however, it had changed completely. The saloon bar still offered tradition, but the lounge had morphed into a reception area and smart cocktail bar for the restaurant, now housed in a striking conservatory extension.

There were no great surprises on the menu, but the freshness of the ingredients and excellent cooking had earned the pub favourable mentions in the county magazine and various food guides and, even early in the week as this was, there were few empty tables to be seen.

The staff were mainly locals, and they all seemed genuinely pleased to see Chloe, if a little surprised. Ian, she noted with some surprise of her own, was treated as a regular.

'That pork *afelia* you liked last week is on the specials board tonight,' their waitress told him as she showed them to their table, where Chloe was thrilled to find champagne on ice waiting along with the menus.

'Now there's a bit of forward planning,' she teased as their glasses were filled. 'What a terrific thought.'

'Well, I felt something special was called for to celebrate the return of the native.' Ian touched his glass to hers. 'It's great to see you, Clo. It's been a hell of a long time.'

'I know.' She smiled into his eyes. 'But now, I promise you, I'm home for good.'

She paused. 'Unlike, I've discovered, my aunt and uncle, busily transforming the Grange for the market and a major move. Rather a shock to the system, I have to say.'

'It was a surprise to me too,' he admitted. 'But—things change. People move on. It's the way of the world, and Hal's put his heart and soul into the practice for a long time, so he deserves to enjoy his retirement.'

She toyed with the idea of some jokey comment on the lines of, *however it means I'm going to be homeless. Any suggestions?* but decided it was too early in the evening, confining herself to a neutral, 'I'm happy for them too.'

Besides, the lead should definitely come from him, she thought as she sipped her champagne.

She'd played the scene so often in her imagination—hearing him murmur, 'It's so wonderful to have you back with me, darling. Stay for ever,' as he produced the little velvet jeweller's box—that she felt as if she'd somehow missed a cue.

'I think I might try this pork *afelia* you're so keen on,' she said as she scanned the menu. 'With the vegetable terrine to start with.'

'It's a good choice,' he said. 'I had it when I brought Lloyd Hampton, our new partner-to-be here. Wanted to convince him that he wasn't altogether moving away from civilisation as he knows it.'

'It's clearly done the trick.'

'I hope so. He's a really good bloke, and his wife's a doll.'

He's married then? was also going to sound like a sharp elbow in the ribs, thought Chloe.

'I shall look forward to meeting her,' was her chosen alternative.

'You're bound to,' he said. 'I'm pretty sure that Lloyd is interested in buying the Grange. He and Viv have two children, and the third's on the way, so they need the space.'

'Well, yes. It sounds ideal,' said Chloe, resolutely ignoring the pang of disappointment in the far corner of her mind which had visualised a very different future for her old home when she and Ian would also need more space than the cottage. Hopefully for the same reason.

When they took their seats at the corner, candlelit table waiting for them, Ian drank another half glass of champagne, then announced he was switching to mineral water.

'Because you're driving?' Chloe, settling for a glass of house red, gave him a rueful look. 'What a shame, because it's a lovely evening, and we could easily have walked.' *And the cottage is even nearer than the Grange when it's time for home...*

'Past all those twitching curtains?' He pulled a face. 'I'd really rather not. A vehicle at least gives an illusion of privacy.'

'Talking of which,' she said. 'I gather you sold your last jeep to Darius Maynard.'

'I heard he was in the market for something more serviceable in addition to that flashy sports car he's so fond of. I'd decided to trade up, so it seemed like serendipity.'

She said slowly, 'Yes, I suppose so. Although it seems odd—having him back here just as if nothing had happened.'

He shrugged. 'It must have been with his father's agreement, Clo, so it's their family business, not ours.'

'Yes, yes, of course.' She played with a fork. 'I understand Sir Gregory's getting over his stroke.'

'Indeed he is. Coming on by leaps and bounds, according to the latest reports.'

'I'm glad. I always liked him, although he could be intimidating.' She paused. 'I used to go up the Hall when I was in my teens and read to Lady Maynard when she was so ill.'

'How did that happen?'

'I won a school poetry competition that she judged. I enjoyed being with her. She was the sweetest person. Darius was with her a lot too and I always felt that he was secretly her favourite.' She paused. 'I was always glad she didn't know how he turned out. What he did to—Andrew.' She bit her lip. 'Betrayal's such a terrible thing.'

'It is,' Ian said quietly. 'But we don't actually know the circumstances. Maybe they couldn't help themselves.'

Upon which the first course arrived, and the conversation turned inevitably to the food.

And Ian was quite right about the pork, Chloe decided after she'd tasted one of the tender cubes of fillet, flavoured with garlic and coriander, cooked in wine, and served with savoury brown rice and *mangetouts.*

For dessert, she chose an opulent dark-chocolate mousse, well-laced with brandy, while Ian opted for cheese and biscuits.

'You should have picked another pud, so we could share like we used to,' she told him in mock reproach.

He gave a constrained smile. 'Out of practice, I guess.'

For what seemed like the umpteenth time that evening, he took his mobile phone from his pocket and checked it.

And what a very annoying habit that is, thought Chloe as she ate her last spoonful of mousse.

Aloud, she said mildly, 'Isn't Uncle Hal taking your calls this evening?'

'Well, yes.' Ian replaced the phone in his jacket. 'But I'm waiting for news of the Crawfords' Kirsty. She's a really good little bitch—won all kinds of shows already, and this may be her only litter, so it needs to go well.'

Chloe's brows lifted. 'But I thought it had already happened last night.'

'False alarm,' he said. 'Main event still expected at any moment, and they want me to stand by in case of emergency.' He signalled to the waitress. 'Would you like filter coffee or espresso?'

She took a deep breath, summoning up courage she hadn't thought she'd need. 'Why don't we make our minds up about that back at the cottage? It's been a gorgeous meal, but a bit public for a proper reunion, don't you think?' She reached across the table, and touched his hand with hers. 'I really think we need to spend some time alone together—and talk.'

'Yes, of course we should, and I want that too,' Ian said quickly. 'But not tonight, Clo.' He gave an awkward laugh. 'For one thing, the cottage is in a bit of a mess. For another—there's been barely minimum contact between us for a whole year now. I've hardly heard from you, let alone seen you. Being on opposite sides of the country didn't help, either, and both of us being so busy. And now you turning up out of the blue like this is frankly the last thing I was expecting.'

He added quickly, 'It isn't that it's not wonderful to see you, or that I don't want you—please believe that. Just that maybe we should take it easy for a while—get to know each other again—before, well, anything…'

His voice tailed off uncomfortably and in the silence that followed, Chloe could hear her heart beating a sudden tattoo—a call to arms. Because the situation was going terribly, disastrously wrong.

Men go off the boil as quick as they go on it… Mrs Thursgood's words rang ominously in her ears. But that couldn't be happening—not to them…

She removed her hand, and sat back in her chair. Summoned a smile that would somehow manage to be calm and amused at the same time. And give no hint of her inner turmoil of shocked disbelief.

'Actually, you may well be right in wanting not to rush things.' She made herself speak almost casually. 'Being wise for both of us, no less. And, anyway, taking our time could be much nicer. Even exciting.'

She paused. 'Besides, you're clearly up to your ears in work and the new plans for the practice. And I—I have to start looking for another job.

'As for coffee,' she added brightly. 'I think I'd prefer decaf. And when the bill comes, in line with our fresh start, I insist we go Dutch.'

And she stuck to her guns in spite of his obvious reluctance.

Now all I want to do is get out of here, she thought, reaching for her bag, and the blue-and-gold fringed shawl she'd brought instead of a jacket.

But the Fates hadn't finished with her yet.

As she walked back into the bar, the first person she saw was Darius Maynard at a table by the window, talking with apparent intimacy to a girl she'd never seen before, slim and very attractive in a sleeveless red dress, with blonde hair drawn back from her face into a smooth chignon at the nape of her neck

And it seemed Darius had spotted her in return, she thought, her heart sinking as he rose to his feet, smiling faintly.

'What a delightful surprise. Lindsay and I have been to the cinema in East Ledwick and we just popped in for a nightcap. Would you care to join us?'

'It's a kind thought, but I think I'll pass, if you don't mind.' She had no wish to allow any hint of the edgy state of her relationship to become apparent to those shrewd green eyes, currently assessing the deep slash of her neckline. Or expose it to the scrutiny of some strange blonde either. 'Stuff to do tomorrow and all that.'

'But the night is still young,' he said softly. 'So, what about you, Cartwright? Surely you can talk your lady round?'

'On the contrary,' Ian returned, a little frostily. 'Once Chloe's made up her mind, it usually stays that way. And I also have a busy day ahead of me. But thanks again, anyway.'

'I see that leopards don't change their spots,' Chloe commented as they walked to the jeep. 'Who's his latest fancy?'

'Her name's Lindsay Watson,' Ian said shortly. 'And she's his father's resident nurse.'

Aunt Libby's charming girl, thought Chloe and gave a faint whistle. 'Under the same roof, even,' she said lightly. 'How very convenient.'

'Not necessarily.' Ian started the engine. 'He's not irresistible, you know.'

When they reached the Grange, Chloe turned towards him. 'I won't invite you in, but does the fresh start merit a goodnight kiss?' she asked, her voice teasing. 'Or do we just shake hands?'

'Of course I want to kiss you,' he said with sudden roughness. 'Any man would. Hell, even Maynard was looking at you as if he could eat you.'

He pulled her into his arms, his mouth heavy and demanding where she'd expected tenderness—even diffidence. This was the moment she'd been dreaming of—longing for—yet she was struggling to respond, the thrust of his tongue between her parted lips feeling almost—alien.

As his hand pushed aside the edge of her dress to close on her bare breast, she tore her mouth free and sat up abruptly, bracing her hands against his chest in negation.

'Ian—no, please...' she protested hoarsely.

'What's the matter?' He reached for her again. 'Isn't this what you want—what tonight was all about?'

Not like this—never like this…

'But it has to be what we both want. You must see that.' She spoke more calmly, moving back from him, straightening her dress with finality. 'And you—to be honest, I just don't know any more.'

Because suddenly you're a stranger and I don't like it. Can't figure how to deal with it.

There was a silence, then he sighed. 'God, I'm sorry, Clo. You must think I'm insane. I suppose it's being without you for so long. So, can we simply forget tonight and start again?'

His face was looking strained, almost guilty, but perhaps it was a trick of the dim light.

She said quietly, 'That's a good thought.'

He nodded. 'I'll call you tomorrow.'

'Fine.' She paused. 'Then—goodnight.'

As she walked up the path to the door, she heard the jeep start up and drive away and realised her legs were trembling.

'You're back early.' There was music coming from the sitting room where Uncle Hal was relaxing, his paper open at the crossword. 'Have a good time?'

'As always,' she returned cheerfully, lowering herself into the chair opposite. 'What are you listening to?'

'Mozart, of course. A selection of favourite arias, and this is mine starting now.' He turned up the sound a little. 'The Countess lamenting her lost happiness from *Figaro*. *"Dove sono I bei momenti"*.'

'Oh, yes, I remember,' she said slowly. 'When you took Aunt Libby and me to Glyndebourne for her birthday. It was wonderful.' And quoted, '"Where are the beautiful moments of pleasure and delight? Where have they flown, those vows made by a deceitful tongue?"'

He nodded. 'A supreme moment of artistry.'

Then the poignant music and the soaring melancholy of the exquisite soprano voice captured them and held them in silence.

The aria was still in Chloe's head, plangent and heart-wrenching, as she went up to her room.

Maybe not the ideal thing to have listened to in the circumstances, she acknowledged wryly as she got ready for bed.

Yet nothing had really been lost, she thought. They'd just got off to a rocky start, that was all. And somewhere soon, with Ian, she would find that those 'moments of pleasure and delight' hadn't disappeared at all, but were still waiting for her.

It will all be fine, she told herself, turning on her side and closing her eyes. I know it.

CHAPTER FOUR

'I MET Sir Gregory's charming nurse last night,' Chloe remarked, watching her aunt extract a tray of scones from the Aga. 'She was in the Willowford Arms having a drink.'

Aunt Libby shot her a swift glance as she transferred her baking to a cooling rack. 'And you thought—what?'

Chloe shrugged. 'That she seemed intent on charming her patient's son and heir.'

'You mean she was with Darius?' Her aunt's brows lifted.

'Well, they're both single, so why not? Another blonde, like Penny, of course. He runs true to form.' Chloe espied a crumb escaping from the rack and ate it.

'I never noticed he had any particular preference,' her aunt said drily. 'However, Lindsay Watson's a lovely girl as well as being extremely capable with a lot of sense.' She added slowly. 'Darius could do far worse.'

'And often has.' Chloe tried to encourage the edge of another scone to make its bid for freedom and had her hand slapped away.

'Those are for the WI tea, madam. If you're hungry there's plenty of fruit in the bowl.'

'Yes, Auntie dear.' Chloe examined a fleck on her nail. 'But how do you think Sir Gregory would feel about it— Darius and his nurse I mean?'

'Thankful, probably,' Mrs Jackson returned briskly. 'It's

high time that young man married and had a family. It's his duty and exactly what the Hall needs, so it could well be the best thing all round. Besides, it would be good for his father to have grandchildren. Give him a new interest in life. Nurse Swann who helps with some of the night duties says he gets bored, which in turn makes him impatient—and that isn't helping his recovery.'

'No,' Chloe said slowly. 'I can understand that.'

She was less sure about her inner vision of Sir Gregory's stern stateliness under siege from a pack of blond infants.

While the image of Darius the married man was something else again.

Suddenly restive, she reached over to the fruit bowl, took an apple and bit into it. 'I thought I might drive over to East Ledwick later,' she went on casually. 'Call in at that agency that used to find me work when I was on vacation.'

Her aunt turned from the sink, staring at her. 'You said the other night that you were going to have a complete break for a while. Pursue other interests.'

Chloe shrugged. 'That was the idea, but now I've started to wonder if I'll find the other interests quite as interesting as I thought. The fact is I'm simply not used to being idle, and taking Lizbeth's dog for a daily walk, however enjoyable, just isn't going to do it for me.' She smiled at her aunt. 'After all, you don't want me getting bored and impatient too.'

'God forbid,' said Aunt Libby devoutly. 'But on the other hand, there's surely no immediate need to go rushing off in all directions? If you want occupation, you could give me a hand with the Grange project. I've decided to start on the dining room next.' She shook her head. 'I've never liked that wallpaper, it's far too dark.'

'On the other hand,' Chloe suggested. 'Might it not be better to leave a few things for Lloyd and his wife to decide for themselves?'

'Lloyd and his wife?' Mrs Jackson dried her hands. 'What do you mean?'

Chloe dropped her apple core into the waste caddy. 'Ian was saying something about them possibly buying the Grange.'

'Was he really?' Her aunt snorted. 'Well that would entirely depend on their offer. Your uncle and I are looking to maximise an asset here, not oblige Ian and his friends.'

Chloe gasped. 'Aunt Libby—you sound almost sharp.'

'Do I?' The older woman hesitated, smiling ruefully. 'Maybe your return has pointed up just how big an upheaval this move is going to be, and I'm having belated qualms.'

'Then don't,' Chloe ordained severely. 'I think it will be wonderful for you both, and, to prove it, I'd be happy to lend a hand with the decorating.'

Even if it isn't in the way I expected, she added silently, and suppressed a sigh.

She deliberately took Flare on a different route that morning, having no wish to encounter Darius again and have to endure any edged remarks he might make about the previous evening.

On the way back, she called into Sawley's Garage to arrange for her petrol gauge to be fixed.

'Heard you were back,' Tom Sawley commented affably. 'And a sight for sore eyes and no mistake, my dear.' He opened the big ledger that was his version of a computer, ran a finger down the crowded page and nodded.

'Tomorrow afternoon suit you? If I can't fix that gauge, I reckon I can find a new one out the back.'

Chloe hid a smile. Here was something that hadn't changed, she thought, Tom's legendary ability to supply any kind of spare part for any kind of make and model of vehicle. If someone brought in a Model T Ford needing a new running board, he'd probably nod and say, 'Got the very thing out the back.'

It must be like Aladdin's cave out there, she thought as the bell above the office door tinkled to announce a new arrival. Giving a casual glance over her shoulder, she saw Lindsay Watson had come in, neat in a navy skirt and white blouse. Beside her, Flare got to her feet with a little whimper of welcome.

Chloe put a restraining hand on her head. 'Sit, good girl.' She smiled at Lindsay. 'Hi, there. We were almost introduced last night. I'm Chloe Benson.'

The other flushed slightly. 'Yes, so Mr Maynard said.' Her voice was low and pleasant but held a note of constraint. 'I'm Sir Gregory's nurse, as I expect you also know.'

'Well, yes.' Chloe found the response curiously distancing, maybe deliberately so. Clearly the famous charm was not universally applied.

She turned back to Mr Sawley. 'Thanks, Tom, tomorrow it is. I'll drop the car off around two-ish.'

Heading for the door, she had to keep a tight hold on Flare who was eagerly pulling at her leash, trying to get to the newcomer, her tail wagging furiously.

'I'm sorry about this,' she said rather breathlessly. 'I hope you don't mind dogs.'

'I haven't had much to do with them,' Lindsay Watson said, stepping back.

Now that, Chloe thought indignantly, really was a snub. Practising for the day when she became the new Lady Maynard, no doubt, but totally misjudging her performance.

Pity you never met your predecessor, she addressed Miss Watson silently as she left. Because she was the warmest, kindest woman.

'While you,' she told Flare, who was still looking back and whining at the closed office door, 'are no judge of character.'

She felt an odd disappointment. She'd enjoyed the time she'd spent with Tanya, and having someone of her own age in Willowford to shop and socialise with occasionally would have been pleasant too. Yet it was clearly not to be.

Maybe Lindsay Watson was simply protecting her territory, Chloe thought, trying to be charitable, when, with Flare safely restored to her owner, she walked back to the Grange.

Perhaps she'd resented the threat of last night's *tête-à-tête* with Darius being interrupted by other company, especially when it included another female.

Well, you're way off track there, lady, she muttered under her breath. I made it clear that it wasn't my idea. I'm not poaching on those preserves, even in my worst nightmare. If you can get him, you're surely welcome to him.

And I won't tell Aunt Libby that her idol has feet of clay.

The home-made cakes at the Tea Rooms were in a category all their own, Chloe told herself as she tried to finish the last few crumbs of her chosen coffee and walnut confection without actually scraping the pattern off the plate, with 'spoiled for choice' and 'to die for' being the phrases that came most readily to mind.

It was market day in East Ledwick and she and Aunt Libby had spent over two hours trawling the fabric stalls seeking curtain material for the newly decorated dining room.

But when Mrs Jackson decided that the design she'd seen at the first stall was the best of the bunch, Chloe had sagged visibly.

Her aunt had patted her shoulder. 'Duty nobly done, dearest. Go and revive yourself with tea and major calories, and I'll meet you by the War Memorial at four o'clock.'

Chloe had obeyed with a thankful heart.

Mrs Jackson was a perfectionist, so it had been a tough week, with layers of old paper to be removed, the plaster beneath restored to a smooth finish, and the paintwork scrubbed down with sugar soap. All of which had taken a mind-boggling amount of time.

But the finished effect of warm sand-coloured walls combined with the brilliant white of the ceiling and cornices made Chloe's conviction that her pores would be permanently clogged with dust seem unimportant. It was a job well done, she realised with satisfaction.

And the new curtains, which the Jacksons would eventually take with them to their new home, were going to look magnificent too.

Work had proved a boon in other ways too, she thought as she drank the rest of her tea. It had given her the chance for some reflection, her relationship with Ian heading the list of potential topics.

She had somehow to overcome her disappointment with the way things had initially turned out between them. And, realistically, she had to shoulder much of the blame for it too.

She'd been hell-bent on earning big money in the short term, even though Ian had made it clear he didn't share her views.

And he was right, she'd told herself soberly. My real focus should have been on the two of us. He saw that. Why the hell couldn't I?

Instead I let the job absorb me so much that Willowford began to seem like a dream world. That I almost forgot there were real people living here who also needed my attention—and my presence.

I should have fought infinitely harder for my time off, concentrated more on maintaining my contact with my home rather than banking the Armstrongs' bonuses for indulging their never-ending demands.

If there was a problem, they threw money at it, and I let them. Stupid, stupid, stupid. Greedy too.

But now she had the chance to make amends. She'd seen Ian twice in the past week, each time for a quiet drink, deliberately ensuring that the atmosphere was more companionable than approaching any form of intimacy.

He hadn't yet asked her back to the cottage, but she wasn't pushing for it either.

Slow and steady, she thought. That's what wins the race.

She reached for the bill, picked up her bag and headed for the cash desk. As she reached it, the street door opened and Lindsay Watson came in. She stood for a moment, her eyes restlessly scanning the busy room, then she saw Chloe and her face seemed to freeze.

What is her problem? Chloe asked herself, exasperated, as she put a tip in the saucer provided, and the rest of the change in her purse.

She forced herself to smile politely. 'Good afternoon, Miss Watson. Looking for someone?'

'Oh—no,' the other girl returned quickly. 'I just wanted some tea.' She glanced round again. 'I didn't realise it would be so crowded.'

'It usually is—especially on market day. But my table's still free over in the corner.'

'Thank you, but perhaps I won't bother. I'm in rather a hurry.' Her attempt at a smile appeared an even greater struggle than Chloe's had been. 'Well—goodbye.'

She whisked out, and by the time Chloe reached the street, she was nowhere to be seen.

I hope she's a damned good nurse, Chloe muttered under her breath, because in other respects, she's seriously weird.

She was too early for her rendezvous with her aunt, and had no shopping of her own, so she decided to spend the time usefully by calling in at the employment agency.

The manager, however, was polite but brisk. 'We have no vacancies in your particular field at the moment, Miss

Benson. People locally are tending to cut back on their higher paid domestic staff because of the economic situation.'

She paused. 'It's a pity you gave up your last position without checking the situation first, and I have to say it might be easier for you to find permanent work in London.'

Which was just what she didn't want to hear, Chloe thought as she emerged, dispirited, into the sunshine.

'Back on the job market, Miss Benson? I'm astonished.'

An all-too-familiar mocking drawl stopped her dead in her tracks. She took a deep breath and turned to see Darius Maynard coming out of the neighbouring ironmongery wearing the close-fitting denim jeans and matching shirt which seemed to have become his uniform these days.

She lifted her chin and met his gaze. 'I fail to see why. Some of us have to toil for our crusts, Mr Maynard,' she retorted. 'We don't all have an income for life dropped into our laps.'

His brows lifted. 'I thought matrimony was about to supply that for you.'

'Then you were wrong,' she told him curtly. 'It doesn't work like that any more.'

'Excuse me if I don't offer my sympathy, sweetheart,' he said. 'Because, believe it or not, I too earn my keep, and have done so for some considerable time.'

'By gambling, I suppose,' Chloe said scornfully. 'As in the old days.' And shut her mind, shuddering inwardly, to the memory of those rumours about illegal dog fights.

'In various ways,' he returned, apparently unperturbed. 'For a while, I worked as a stockman in Australia. I've also helped to train racehorses in Kentucky, and latterly I've been running a vineyard in the Dordogne. All perfectly respectable occupations even by your unflinching standards,' he added, the green eyes a challenge. 'Would you like a copy of my CV?'

He paused, and gave a sharp sigh of irritation. 'Or alternatively shall we stop bitching at each other in this ludicrous way and remember that we used to call each other by our given names? That at one time we were something like friends?'

She felt an odd stillness descend, as if the grumble of the passing traffic and the noise from the market had suddenly faded to a great distance. As if she was entangled in some web which would not allow her to move. To walk away as she wished to do. As she knew she must.

Instead of standing there, as if she was frozen to the spot, looking back at him...

Somewhere a vehicle backfired with a noise like a pistol shot, and with that the world returned. Including her power of speech.

'Were we?' she demanded tautly. 'I really don't remember.'

He stared at her, his eyes narrowing, then shrugged. He said expressionlessly, 'As you wish.' He paused again. 'I note you haven't been up to the stables as I suggested. Am I to take it that your dislike of me is so fixed that you even refuse to exercise my horse?'

She said, 'I've been busy, helping my aunt. Why don't you ask your girlfriend—the one you were with the other night?'

He said flatly, 'Because she's at the Hall to look after my father.'

'Not this afternoon. A little while ago she was looking for you at the Tea Rooms.'

'Was she?' He looked past her, frowning a little. 'Anyway, I don't think she rides,' he added abruptly. 'Or certainly not well enough to handle Orion.'

'And I do?'

He sighed. 'You know it, Chloe. Don't play games. And I'll make a deal with you. Warn me in advance when you're coming and I'll make sure I'm at the other end of the estate. How about that?'

He looked at her rigid expression and his mouth tightened. 'Will you at least think about it?'

'Yes,' she said, staring at the pavement. 'I—I'll think about it.'

But would she? Chloe wondered as she walked back towards the War Memorial. She'd thought about a great deal over the past days as she'd scraped, peeled, filled and painted, but Darius Maynard and the situation at the Hall had not been on her chosen list of subjects. On the contrary, she'd been careful to exclude both of them.

They did not concern her or the life she had planned for herself. They never had. So she shouldn't consider even the most marginal of involvement.

That, she told herself, would be a serious error of judgement.

The box marked 'Clothing' was stacked on top of the others in the attic. Instantly accessible, Chloe thought wryly as she lifted it down. As if it was waiting for me.

The weight alone told her what it contained—her jodhpurs, boots and hard hat, along with a shirt and a couple of elderly sweaters. None of it worn for years. Yet still retained for no good reason.

In fact she'd hoped against hope that the whole lot might also have been consigned to a charity shop or jumble sale by now as part of the de-clutter, but no such luck.

No sign of moths in anything either—not on Aunt Libby's watch.

She unfolded the jodhpurs and studied them critically. They probably won't fit me, she thought. Not after this length of time. After all, I'm hardly some slip of a girl any more.

And I've no intention of splurging on new kit—so, the

problem, which has no actual right to be a problem anyway, could be solved.

But the jodhpurs still hugged her slim hips and long legs as if they loved them. No valid excuse there then, she thought, biting her lip.

The blue shirt, however, strained across the increased fullness of her breasts, and she stared at her reflection with suddenly shadowed eyes, tracing the mother-of-pearl buttons with a fingertip.

This, she told herself, I should definitely not have kept.

Using both hands, she dragged open the front with one swift, almost violent gesture, tearing the buttons from the fabric and rendering the shirt completely unwearable, then dropped it into the waste basket.

And that, she whispered to herself, is the end of that.

'You took your time,' said Arthur. 'Been expecting you all week.'

He led Orion, tacked up and with his ears pricked in anticipation, out of his box and into the yard.

'And Mr Darius said to let you know he was over to Warne Cross this morning to look at the new plantation.' He sent Chloe a sideways look. 'Thinking of riding over there, was you?'

'No.' Chloe swung herself up into the saddle and waited while Arthur adjusted her stirrups. 'I thought I'd hack him round the park for a while, then take him up onto the hill.'

'He'll carry you right wherever you go and that's a fact.' Arthur ran an affectionate hand over the gelding's neck. 'Mr Darius got him in France. Had him shipped over. Great lad, aren't you? Plenty of spirit, but good-hearted with it.'

He sniffed. 'Unlike that other contrary devil in there,' he added, jerking his head towards the stable. 'God knows why Mr Andrew ever bought 'un. Could've broken his neck on him any day of the week. Didn't need to go climbing no mountain.'

'But Andrew was a good rider.' Chloe soothed Orion who had begun to sidle a little, impatient to be off.

'Fair,' Arthur said grudgingly. 'Not a patch on his brother. Took too many damned risks. Told him so, many a time, but made no damned difference.'

He paused. 'But I'm glad to see you round here again, Chloe gal. Good seat you always had and nice steady hands. You and this boy will get on fine, I reckon.'

'Or he'll come home without me,' Chloe sent him a grin, then turned Orion towards the archway.

But that was never going to happen. Orion attempted to take a few serious liberties in their early acquaintance, but soon realised the girl on his back would not allow such behaviour and decided to settle for mutual enjoyment instead.

And when they reached the long, straight stretch on top of the hill and Chloe gave him his head at last, she could have shouted her exhilaration to the skies as Orion flew along.

She cantered him slowly home, the pair of them in total amity. She'd been out for considerably longer than she'd planned and, as she walked him back under the archway, she expected to find Arthur waiting for them and began to frame an apology, but the yard was empty.

Not that it mattered, she thought. In the old days, she'd have done her own unsaddling and seen to her horse's comfort as a matter of course. She could do the same now.

As she got Orion settled and refilled his water bucket, she could hear restless movements from the box opposite and found a pair of glittering dark eyes in a handsome black head with a white blaze watching her with suspicion.

So this was Samson, she thought, feeling a stir of interest and excitement. Big with powerful shoulders and quarters, he certainly lived up to his name.

Chloe spoke to him softly, saying his name and he backed away, nostrils flaring.

She went a little closer. 'Beauty,' she crooned. 'Gorgeous boy. What's the matter, then?'

'Not a great deal. He's simply wondering how to get you near enough to take a piece out of your arm,' Darius said from the doorway. 'I don't advise you give him the opportunity.'

It was Chloe's turn to step backwards. She said with faint breathlessness, 'I thought you were at Warne Cross.'

'I have been,' he said tersely. 'But I realised I couldn't hang around there all day, even to oblige you. As it was, I was asking Crosby so many stupid questions, he must have thought I was losing my mind.'

He came in. Stood, blocking her path to the door. 'Arthur having his lunch?'

'I suppose he must be.' She turned hurriedly to pick up the saddle from the door of Orion's box. 'I—I'll just take this over to the tack room.'

'Leave it,' he said. 'I'll do it later.'

'It's no trouble—really.'

He said with faint amusement, 'Or at least it's the kind of trouble you can handle. Isn't that what you actually mean? But you have no need to worry, sweetheart. After all, you're sacrosanct. Promised to another in the shape of our worthy junior vet.'

'And that's supposed to be some safeguard?' The words were out before she could stop them. 'Your brother didn't find it so.'

'No,' he said very quietly. 'He didn't.' He paused. 'Perhaps you shouldn't have reminded me of that salient fact—and particularly not here. And not now.'

There was another of those odd intense silences. Chloe had the odd impression that she could hear the rush of blood through her veins. The whisper of the breath she was holding.

'I'm sorry.' Her voice was small, husky. 'I had no right to say that. No reason either.'

'No?' Darius asked. He took a step nearer. 'Can you put your hand on your heart and swear that?'

She swallowed. 'I've apologised. That should be enough.'

'Enough?' he repeated. 'That's a paltry kind of word, Chloe, when you consider some of the memories we share.'

She lifted her chin, her heart going like a trip hammer. 'I only remember a girl, little more than a child, who once nearly made a fool of herself and was only saved from a life-time of regret because you remembered just in time that you wanted another man's woman far more.

'You were a disaster that didn't happen, Darius. That's all. So let's not pretend anything else.' She took a breath. 'And if you come any closer, I warn you I'm going to scream until Arthur and everyone else in the household hears me and comes running.'

For a moment, he was very still, then he moved ostentatiously to one side, leaning against the door of an empty box.

As she walked past him, staring rigidly in front of her, he said quietly, 'One day, darling, you're going to realise you're the one who's pretending. And when you do, I shall be waiting.' He paused. 'See you around.'

And to Chloe, trying desperately not to run to her car, his words were a threat, not a promise.

CHAPTER FIVE

'NEVER again.' Chloe hit the steering wheel with clenched fists, her words grating through gritted teeth. 'Never again.'

She'd headed for one of her favourite spots, driving pretty much on autopilot. But having arrived there and parked on the short grass, she found the car suddenly seemed confining, claustrophobic. She flung open her door and almost scrambled out, standing for a moment, drawing deep breaths of the warm, still air to calm herself.

Ahead of her, the ground sloped away down to where the Willow, glinting in the sunlight, pursued its leisurely course down the valley. She walked slowly down the narrow track towards the water until she came to a large flat boulder a few yards from the bank, and climbed up onto its smooth surface, resting her chin on her drawn-up knees.

How many times, she wondered, had she cycled out here over the years, to swim in the deep calm pool under the trees a few yards downstream, then sunbathe stretched out on this same rock?

But maybe she'd chosen the wrong refuge today, she thought, gazing unseeingly at the view. After all, this was also where she'd always come to think, not escape from her thoughts.

Besides, it held altogether too many memories, reminding her that once she'd been tempted into a dangerous, impossible dream that had no place in the kind of life she'd envisaged for herself. A dream from which, thankfully, she'd been swiftly and brutally awoken.

And the intervening years had only reinforced that awakening, teaching her to concentrate on a future that would provide stability as well as true happiness. The things, she told herself, that she'd grown up with, and which were what really mattered in life. So in a way, the past had taught her a valuable lesson.

Yet ever since she'd come back, she'd had the disturbing sensation that everything was changing, and that, in some strange way, the ground was being cut away from under her feet.

If I'd known that Darius was here, I'd never have come back, Chloe thought, closing her eyes. Or, at least, not to stay. I thought the past was safely buried, so how could I have guessed?

Well maybe by reading Aunt Libby's letters properly and asking the right follow-up questions, she thought, biting her lip with swift savagery. Only I didn't and now I have to live with the consequences—but perhaps not permanently.

She wondered restively just how committed Ian was to Willowford. If it wasn't too late to persuade him that they should also embark on a new start together somewhere completely different. But, naturally, he would want to know why, and what explanation could she possibly offer that would make some kind of sense without involving any potential damaging admissions?

Those vows made by a deceitful tongue...

The Countess Almaviva's words once more wound their sad way through her mind and her throat tightened.

Except, of course, there had been no vows of any kind.

In fact, nothing happened with Darius, she assured herself with a kind of desperation. Nothing. Not then. Not now.

But it could have done so easily. So terribly, even fatally easily. And I can never let myself forget that. Not for a single, solitary moment.

So why on earth did I go within a mile of the Hall today? Why did I believe he'd keep his distance and let myself succumb to the temptation to ride his beautiful horse? Didn't the events of seven years ago teach me anything? And, if so, why didn't I see what was coming?

However, she thought, pushing a hand through her dishevelled hair, Darius's behaviour does suggest a reason for Lindsay Watson's hostility. Something may have been said or merely implied which has caused her to see me as some kind of rival.

And I can't even take her on one side and say, 'Look, frankly, you've got hold of the wrong end of the stick. If you want the glamorous Mr Maynard, have him and good luck to you, because you'll need it.'

Especially, she reminded herself quickly, when no-one seems to know if Penny is completely out of the picture, or simply waiting in the wings, and found she was suddenly shivering in spite of the warmth of the day.

She slipped down from the rock and walked back to the car.

She didn't want to be alone, she thought as she started the engine. She wanted to adjust her focus back to the things that mattered, therefore she needed to see Ian, to sit with him and talk quietly like they used to. Like they should still be doing, because surely, by now, it was time they began to formulate some plans, even if they weren't the ones she'd had in mind when she returned?

Maybe we could both work abroad, she thought suddenly. I could suggest that to him—make it sound like an adventure. Establish completely new roots before we start a family.

But for that I need to see him face to face. Convince him it's not just some crazy whim.

It occurred to her that he usually went back to the cottage for his lunch break if he wasn't too busy. Maybe instead of continuing to wait patiently for an invitation which seemed a very long time in coming, she should simply pay him a surprise visit.

I'd have done it a year ago without thinking twice, she thought. So why not now? *Carpe diem*, as the saying is. Seize the day.

But there was no sign of Ian's jeep on the patch of waste ground by his fence where he normally parked. And the door and windows were all firmly closed.

Chloe gave a small defeated sigh. She'd already turned the car to head back towards the Grange when some impulse made her switch off the engine and get out. While she was here, she thought, she might as well take another look at her future home, even if it was to be only temporary, and, at the same time, see for herself the kind of chaos Ian seemed content, if apologetic, to live in.

It couldn't go on, of course, she told herself with mock-sternness. She would have to take the situation in hand at some point, especially if he went along with her idea of a move and agreed to put the place on the market.

The kitchen and dining room were at the front of the house, with the sitting room, and Ian's office at the back, overlooking the small garden.

Bracing herself, Chloe decided to face the kitchen first, always supposing its windows were clean enough to look through, she added silently, wrinkling her nose.

But the panes were surprisingly grime-free, offering an uninterrupted view of the room beyond. Eyes widening, Chloe saw a row of herbs in pots on the windowsill, a new Belfast sink, crockery neatly set out on a small dresser, a gleaming white cooker and a square pine table with a bowl of fruit at its centre. And the room wasn't just tidy, she thought. It looked clean too. And herbs? She'd thought scrambled eggs represented the height of Ian's culinary ambitions.

The dining room told the same story, with an oak table, six chairs and a matching sideboard all neatly set out. None of them new, admittedly, and certainly not antique, either, but all gleaming with polish. And on the table this time two pottery candle-holders and a vase of flowers.

Chloe stepped back, frowning in bewilderment. What on earth had Ian been talking about? she asked herself. Because if this was a mess, then the Grange must be a pigsty. None of it made any sense.

She walked slowly round to the back of the house. The sitting room boasted a cream leather sofa and a matching recliner, neither of which she'd seen before, and the office with its desk, computer and filing cabinet was a picture of order.

So what had happened to all the cheerful squalor she'd been expecting?

She could only think he'd been overcome by guilt and hired a team of industrial cleaners to sort him out. But they would only do the basics. It must be Ian's own efforts that had made the cottage look so homelike and cosy.

I told Tanya I wanted to surprise him, she thought wryly. He must have been thinking on the same lines, and he's certainly succeeded. I'm the most surprised female in Willowford. And when I'm asked to pay my official visit, I'll jump for joy and praise him lavishly.

It was how she'd always visualised the cottage. Just how she'd wanted it to be, apart, possibly, from the cream leather seating, but perhaps that was a man thing. Yet she'd played no part in its transformation.

And while it was undoubtedly carping and churlish to feel disappointed over this, somehow she couldn't help herself.

I just wish he'd told me what he was planning, she thought restively. She wondered what improvements and modernisation had been carried out upstairs, but she'd need a ladder to find out, and anyway she was almost relieved not to know.

The house seemed to be beckoning to her—inviting her to enter and share its welcoming charm—but it was securely locked, and there was no way in, she thought, rattling at the handle of the back door in sudden frustration.

Her future home—and she was excluded. As if she was merely an outsider condemned to remain on the other side of a few panes of glass, looking in.

And, while she knew she was totally overreacting, she could not prevent this disturbing thought accompanying her all the way back to the Grange.

Where another unwelcome surprise awaited her.

'An invitation,' said Aunt Libby. 'Dinner at the Hall, no less. It used to be a regular occurrence, of course, when Lady Maynard was alive,' she went on. 'But rather fell into abeyance afterwards. I suppose these occasions really need a hostess, and Andrew's wife never gave the impression she was keen on indulging the locals. The Birthday Ball was as far as she was prepared to go, and that turned out to be the last, of course.'

'Yes.' Chloe bit her lip as she looked down at the note in Darius's imperious and unmistakable black handwriting.

And now, she thought, the Hall has a hostess again...

She took a swift, uneven breath. 'What excuse can we possibly give?'

'Don't be silly, dear,' her aunt returned briskly. 'This is the equivalent of a royal summons. I gather from Mrs Vernon, who brought the note round herself, that Sir Gregory is now well enough to see visitors, which is really good news, although he won't actually be joining us for the meal.'

'Well, I can't go,' Chloe insisted stubbornly. 'Ian and I have plans for next Wednesday.'

'Then you'll have to change them,' Mrs Jackson said firmly. 'Ian's also being invited, and as the Hall is a client of the practice, he certainly won't refuse. He can't afford to. And nor can we. Something you have to learn when you're in business in a small community.'

She shook her head at Chloe's mutinous expression. 'For heaven's sake, my girl, it's only a couple of hours or so out of your life, and Mrs Denver is still a superlative cook. What on earth is your problem?'

One, Chloe thought bleakly, that I cannot possibly share.

She shrugged. 'Perhaps I'm not very interested in the rehabilitation of Darius Maynard. I imagine this is what it's all about.'

He'd told her himself he intended to become a good neighbour, so maybe she should have seen this coming.

I'm being manipulated again, she thought, bitterly. And I don't like it.

So it was almost a comfort to know that Lindsay Watson would probably like it even less.

'Well, it's only to be expected, as he's the heir apparent. And if his father can accept the situation, who are we to quibble?' Aunt Libby paused.

'Besides, he was very young when it all happened, and we all do foolish things that we regret when we're young.'

Twenty-five, thought Chloe. He was twenty-five. Just as I am now.

She said expressionlessly, 'I suppose so.'

But I don't intend to regret anything. Not again. Never again...

Ian took her to East Ledwick that evening, to a small bistro that had recently opened to considerable acclaim.

'One of these evenings, you'll have to cook for me yourself,' she said, scanning the menu appreciatively.

'Have a heart, Clo. You know my limitations,' Ian said as he summoned the wine waiter and ordered a bottle of Rioja.

All evidence to the contrary, thought Chloe.

Aloud, she said lightly, 'I'm no longer sure you have any—something I find very intriguing.'

She paused. 'So, how do you think our renewed acquaintance is progressing?'

He flushed a little. 'What do you mean?'

Once again, it was hardly the response she'd hoped for, but Chloe persevered.

'I was thinking that maybe it was time we began to consider the future again. To talk about what we both want from life.'

He fiddled with his cutlery. 'I guess we should. Sooner or later.'

He was not, she thought, making it easier for her.

She said, 'Would it help if I told you I was wrong to take that job? To spend so much time away from here?'

'You had your reasons, Clo. You wanted to earn big money fast. No-one can blame you for that.'

'But it's as if I've come back to a different world,' she said. 'One that I don't understand.'

'Well, nothing stands still. Circumstances change. People change.' He smiled awkwardly. 'You're probably not the same person who went away either.'

'But that's what I came back to be,' she said slowly. 'I thought you knew that.'

He was about to answer when he looked past her towards the doorway, his gaze sharpening.

He said, 'It seems as if this is the venue of the moment,' and got to his feet.

Chloe did not need to turn her head to know who had just

come in. The butterflies suddenly cartwheeling in her stomach told her all that was necessary.

Oh, God, this can't be happening to me. Not a second time.

'What a very pleasant surprise,' Darius said lightly as he and Lindsay came to stand beside their table. She was wearing black tonight, a shade that set off her blond hair and pale skin, making her look oddly ethereal. He was totally casual in chinos with a dark red, open-necked shirt, and a light cashmere jacket slung over one shoulder, yet, at the same time, managed in some mysterious way to make every other man in the room look ordinary. 'Why don't we join forces—with you as my guests naturally?'

Chloe could think of all kinds of reasons and was sure that his companion could double the number, but as her lips parted in startled negation, she was instantly checked by Ian's stiffly uttered, 'Thank you, we'd be delighted.'

Aunt Libby's wise words about business and small communities nudged at her brain, as she rose silently to accompany them to a larger table, but surely there were limits?

Although they had apparently ceased to apply, she thought when, inevitably, she found herself placed directly opposite Darius.

She concentrated her attention ferociously on the menu, trying not to listen as he moved effortlessly into charming host mode, offering his enthusiastic approval of Ian's choice of wine when it appeared at the table.

I could always invent a headache and ask to be taken home, she thought, *but he'd know I was lying, and that I was actually running away again. And that would be even worse than having to sit here with my feet tucked under my chair to avoid even the slightest accidental contact with him.*

Indifference is what I should aim for, with a slight frosting of annoyance at this unwarranted intrusion on my tête-à-

tête. Especially as Ian and I seemed to be getting somewhere at last.

She smothered a sigh and asked for smoked salmon and a fillet steak, medium rare, conventional and easy.

'Is this your first visit here?' Ian was asking.

Darius shook his head. 'I came to the opening. The owner's a friend of mine—Jack Prendergast.' He looked across at Chloe, who no longer had a menu to shelter behind. 'Maybe you remember him from the last Birthday Ball? Large guy with red hair, rarely without a smile.'

She drank some water. 'I really don't recall much about that evening at all.' She spoke coolly, and saw the green eyes spark with swift amusement.

'What a shame,' he said softly. 'I'm sure he hasn't forgotten you. Clearly I'll have to make the next ball rather more memorable.'

She stared at him, instant embarrassment yielding as quickly to shock. 'You mean you're planning to revive it?' Her voice sounded hoarse. 'But why?'

'Because it seems a good—a neighbourly thing to do.' He gave her a faint smile. 'And it might also lay a few ghosts to rest. My father would like that.'

But how can that possibly happen, she thought, when everyone present will know that twenty-four hours later you ran away with your brother's wife?

'I wasn't around for the last one,' Ian said. 'Why is it called the Birthday Ball?'

'In memory of my great-great grandmother Lavinia,' Darius returned. 'She was a celebrated nineteenth-century beauty, fancied by the Prince of Wales, among others, and her doting husband, to whom she was entirely faithful, decided to mark her birthday at the end of July with a gala dance at the Hall each year.

'People came to it from all over the country,' he added.

'And subsequent generations continued the tradition, although they didn't cast their net for guests quite as wide. By my mother's time, it was pretty much confined to local people. But it was always a great night.'

How can you say that? Chloe demanded silently. When you know what you did—how you ruined people's lives? How can you live with yourself?

She said quietly, 'Won't Sir Gregory find it rather— taxing?'

'On the contrary, he's all for it.' It was Lindsay who replied. 'He gets very bored, and the arrangements for the ball will hopefully give him a new interest.'

Well, you're his nurse, thought Chloe, so you of all people should know. Or are you more concerned with being the belle of the ball and opening the dancing in Darius's arms? Have you already moved being Lady Maynard?

She said expressionlessly, 'Amen to that,' and drank some of her wine.

The arrival of the first course made things marginally easier, because the food could be discussed in place of trickier subjects.

Chloe made herself eat every scrap of her smoked salmon, while Darius cheerfully demolished a fair chunk of coarse pâté, but Lindsay treated her goat's cheese tartlet as if arsenic might be one of the ingredients and Ian seemed equally hesitant over his potted shrimps.

Listen, she addressed the pair of them silently, you may be no happier about the way this evening is going than I am, but why let it show? Let him play whatever game this is, and pretend that it doesn't matter to you. Or simply treat it as a rehearsal for dinner at the Hall.

'So,' Ian said, as their plates were being cleared. 'How's Samson these days? Still bent on self-destruction?' He turned to Chloe. 'I had to attend to his damaged hock when he tried to kick his way out of his box a few months ago. We had to sedate him to get near him.'

Darius shrugged a shoulder. 'He's the same evil-tempered swine that he ever was. But his malevolence is directed more towards the rest of the world these days. He scares Arthur stiff.'

He paused. 'However, he's seriously fast and he jumps like an angel, so I'm considering letting him put all that ferocious energy to some good use by sending him over to stud in Ireland.' He gave a swift grin. 'A few good-looking mares may give him a better outlook on life.'

'My sympathies are with the mares,' said Chloe tartly, and his smile widened.

'I wouldn't expect anything different,' he told her softly, and she sat back in her chair wishing she hadn't spoken.

A little later, it occurred to her, as she ate a steak so tender she could probably have cut it with her fork, that Ian and she could quite easily be married and on their honeymoon by the date of the Birthday Ball, which would solve a multitude of problems. It was something to aim for anyway.

And when the meal from hell was over and they were finally alone, she would convince Ian that she was entirely his. Go into his arms with tenderness and passion, and give him everything he'd ever wanted from her.

She thought of him kissing her, his mouth warm as it brushed her eyes, her cheeks, her parted eager lips. Of his teeth tugging gently at the lobe of her ear, as his fingertips stroked her throat, moving downwards with slow, exquisite deliberation.

Of him touching her at last, his hands gentle on her breasts, lingering on her thighs, making her body arc towards him in unspoken longing.

And his voice, husky with desire: 'Oh, God, my sweet, my angel, do you know what you're doing to me?'

For a moment, she felt her body flare with the fierce heat of arousal, her face burn in the voluptuous anticipation of pleasure.

She felt her entire being quiver into a sigh, then looked up and saw Darius watching her across the table, his eyes like emeralds in the candlelight, his gaze intent—rapt. Saw the faint, sensuous curve of his mouth, and the almost idle play of his fingers on the stem of his wineglass.

She realised with horror exactly whose caresses she was remembering. Whose lovemaking she had once invited with such total candour.

And, worst of all, knew that he knew it too. That he had read her every thought. Shared each memory. Recognised every secret need.

Leaving her, she thought, defenceless.

For a moment, the space between them seemed to crackle as if charged with electricity.

Chloe's hand moved in hasty, instinctive negation and caught the edge of her own glass, spilling its contents in a ruby flood across the white tablecloth.

'Oh, God, I'm so sorry. I can't believe I've been so clumsy. What a total mess. Shouldn't we put salt on it—or white wine?'

She was on her feet, babbling apologies to everyone, including the waiter who mounted an efficient and smiling rescue operation, removing all the empty plates, replacing the cloth with a clean one, and bringing fresh cutlery and glasses along with the dessert menus.

When Ian tried to pour some more wine for her, she refused. 'I think I've had more than enough, don't you? We don't want them adding in the laundry bill.' Smiling, making a joke of it, but with determination. Wanting to make the silent man on the other side of the table believe it was only alcohol which had set her aglow. And that anything else was entirely in his imagination.

Emphasising this by asking ruefully for black coffee instead of pudding. Then, by moving fractionally closer to Ian and touching his sleeve with a teasing fingertip. By taking a few grapes, a sliver of celery and some fragments of Stilton from his plate. Intimate gestures, she thought, which should designate precisely who was at the centre of her world. And restore her own equilibrium at the same time.

While Darius lounged in his chair, apparently too enthralled by the colour of the cognac he'd ordered to actually drink it, and his companion, eyes fixed on her plate, ate her way doggedly through a *crème brûlée*.

When Ian looked at his watch and spoke apologetically about having an early start in the morning, there was no demur from anyone. Darius simply nodded and signalled for the bill.

Outside on the pavement, there were the usual awkward moments of leave-taking, coupled with over-hearty expressions of gratitude from Ian.

Lindsay was the first to turn away, walking rapidly up the street to where Darius's car was parked.

He smiled at them as he prepared to follow her. 'Well,' he said softly. 'That was most enjoyable. I shall look forward once again to welcoming you to the Hall next week.'

On the surface, it was the polite—the conventional—thing to say.

But Chloe knew differently. She recognised the veiled threat beneath the formal courtesy, and she stood, trembling inside, as she watched him go.

And as she sat without speaking beside the equally silent

Ian on the homeward journey, one desperate question echoed and re-echoed in her brain. *What am I going to do? Dear God, what am I going to do?*

CHAPTER SIX

CHLOE found sleep elusive that night.

She had made no attempt to resume her interrupted conversation with Ian when they arrived back at the Grange. She'd felt obliged to offer him more coffee, but was thankful when he declined the suggestion, and after a swift, almost clumsy, peck on the lips, drove off, saying he'd call her.

Her aunt and uncle were intent on a game of Scrabble when she put her head round the sitting room door and wished them goodnight, so she was able to escape to her room without Aunt Libby's eagle eye spotting there was anything amiss.

But she couldn't hide from herself, or the turmoil raging inside her. She turned restlessly in the bed, seeking a cool place on the pillow, even the sheet seeming to press her down.

Eventually, she pushed it aside and got up, pulling on her cotton robe before making her way over to the window seat. There was no breeze coming through the open window, and the moon looked huge and heavy above the fields, a great golden orb preparing to drop out of the sky.

Chloe leaned back against the wall, closing her eyes.

She'd thought it was all over and done with long ago. That she'd relegated the past to some forgotten corner of her mind. Conquered her demons and laid them to rest.

Now it seemed she had to confront them again—one last time.

But it has to stop here, she told herself. I can't allow some ludicrous, meaningless memory to interfere with the life I've chosen for myself—everything I've planned for and worked towards for the last seven years.

I won't allow it.

I deal with it here and now, and then I let it go. For ever.

And if there's pain, I deal with that too.

It had been the same hot, still weather then, she remembered. But oppressive, too, as if an approaching storm was being signalled. And that wasn't simply a dramatic veneer imposed in retrospect by her imagination.

'Off to the Willow Pond again?' Aunt Libby had asked that afternoon so many years ago now, glancing up at the sky. 'In that case, take your waterproof. The weather's going to change.'

'Oh, I'll be back long before that happens,' Chloe had assured her breezily, tucking a towel and some sun lotion into her haversack and slipping her arms through its straps.

If she was honest, she'd been feeling at a bit of a loose end. School was over, and only the results of her public examinations remained, about which she'd been modestly confident. Her best friends Jude and Sandie had both been abroad with their parents on celebratory vacations, and long weeks had stretched ahead of her before the start of the university year.

Worse still, Ian was away assisting on an experimental inoculation programme for cattle in Shropshire, and his regular phone calls were no compensation at all.

At the same time, her woebegone expression had cut very little ice with Aunt Libby, who was kind but frank.

'Yes, he's a thoroughly decent boy, and your uncle and I think the world of him. He's going to make a fine vet and probably a good husband when the time comes, but it's far too soon for either of you to be thinking seriously about anyone.

'Enjoy your salad days, my dear, and fall in and out of love half a dozen times. That's what being young is for. But you also have your degree course to concentrate on, and a career to consider. Don't get sidetracked, however appealing it may seem at the moment.' She paused. 'And don't lead Ian up any garden paths either. He deserves better.'

And what she meant by that was anyone's guess!

It was all right for Aunt Libby, Chloe thought rebelliously later as she cycled through the lanes. She'd probably forgotten what it was like to be turned breathless by the sound of someone's voice, or feel your heart skip a beat when he walked into the room. That is, of course, if she'd ever known. She and Uncle Hal were sweet together, but...

Anyway, she ought to be glad that I've already met the man I want, she told herself. That there's no fear of me plunging off the rails at college, or anywhere else.

In addition to that, she decided with sudden mischief, Aunt Libby should be gratified that her niece had suddenly discovered a strong domestic streak and was taking a real, if unexpected, interest in housework. In learning the unfashionable arts of cooking, cleaning, washing and ironing, and for their own sake too, rather than just with an eye to the future.

Not very liberated, perhaps, but deeply satisfying in its own way. And what was so wrong in preferring order to chaos?

She found the Willow Pond deserted, as it often was midweek. Quickly she stripped to her pale pink bikini and slid down into the cool water, enjoying the sensation of its freshness against her heated skin. She swam to the other side of the pool and back, using a slow and dreamy breaststroke which seemed to lend itself to the general languor of the day.

She hauled herself out and went and sat on the rock where she'd left her towel, wringing the water from her waving mass of dark hair, and combing the damp strands with her fingers as she lifted her face to the sun.

'My God—little Chloe grown up at last. Who'd have thought it?'

The amused masculine drawl made her jump and she turned her head with a start, shading her eyes, her heart thudding as she realised who was standing a few yards away.

She said rather breathlessly, 'Darius—Mr Maynard, I mean. What are you doing here?'

'The same as you. Or that was the plan. And Darius will do just fine.' He walked forward and stood regarding her, hands on hips, the mobile mouth quirking. 'Thinking of changing your own name to Lorelei, my pet?'

She flushed under his scrutiny, suddenly aware just how skimpy her bikini really was and wishing she'd chosen to wear her former school's regulation one-piece swimsuit instead.

Or cycled to the swimming baths in East Ledwick.

She reached hurriedly for her discarded cotton cut-offs and elderly striped shirt, with a silent sigh for the dry underwear in her haversack. 'I—I'll get dressed and out of your way.'

'Please don't,' he said. 'Unless, of course, you want me to feel terminally guilty about driving you off. Surely, there's plenty of room for both of us.' He paused. 'Besides, I thought we were old friends.'

Which was, presumably, some kind of absurd joke, Chloe thought uncertainly. Because she and Darius Maynard were nothing of the kind. He knew her mainly from her reading sessions with his late mother, and on Lady Maynard's instructions had seen her to the main door when they were over, chatting lightly to cover her own tongue-tied silence as she walked beside him.

After that, she'd encountered him a few times when she'd been up at the Hall to exercise one of the old ponies that he and his brother had ridden as boys, and while he'd been perfectly pleasant, she'd always felt uneasy around him, and glad to get away.

But for the past two years she'd hardly seen him at all.

'Working abroad,' Mrs Thursgood had said with a sniff. 'Paid to keep away and out of mischief more like.'

Aunt Libby had uttered a mild remonstration, but Chloe could tell her heart wasn't really in it, and had wondered about the nature of the mischief.

Now, she was no longer a shy schoolgirl, mute in the face of his male sophistication, therefore there was no earthly reason for her to be shaken even marginally by this unexpected meeting.

So why did her mouth feel dry, and how could she account for this strange hollowness in the pit of her stomach? Her new-found poise must be more fragile than she thought, she realised without pleasure.

She said, 'I—I thought you were working away.'

'I have been. I came back yesterday. Thought I'd revisit some people and places. Renew old acquaintances.' His smile teased like the stroke of a hand on her skin. 'And with great good fortune, I find I'm beginning with you.'

He began to unbutton his shirt, and Chloe looked down at her towel, tracing its pattern with a fascinated finger.

She ought to leave, she thought. Make some excuse and—go. He was undoubtedly what Jude's grandmother had once described, eyes dancing from her own young days, as 'NSIT, my dears: Not Safe In Taxis,' reducing them both to gales of laughter. Only now it didn't seem so funny.

And she recalled Sandie, who'd seen him when the local hunt met near her village, had pronounced him 'utterly gorgeous'.

A splash told her that Darius was safely occupied in the pool providing her with the ideal opportunity to make a quick exit. Except that haste of any kind did not recommend itself in this kind of baking heat.

Nor did she wish him to know that he caused her even the slightest alarm, she thought, biting her lip. Especially when there was no reason for it. No reason at all.

She found herself reaching for her sun lotion and smoothing it gently over her arms, shoulders and the first swell of her breasts above the cups of her bikini, before proceeding down to her midriff and the slender length of her legs.

By the time he returned, lithe in black trunks, raking his wet hair back from his face, she was replacing the cap on the bottle.

She said with an assumption of composure, 'Was that good?'

He shook his head. 'Good doesn't come near it. And it may be our last chance for a while. There's thunder in the air. Can't you feel it?'

As he picked up his towel and began to blot the water from his tanned skin, it occurred to Chloe that she was aware of a number of sensations she would have much preferred to ascribe to atmospheric pressure.

At the same time, she realised that, while it was still hot, there was now a dull look to the sky, and the sun was a brazen globe behind a thin veil of cloud.

When he'd finished drying himself, Darius shook out the towel, spread it on the grass and stretched out on it a decorous few feet away from her.

'It's been quite a while, so how's the world treating you, Miss Chloe Benson?' He plucked a grass stalk and began to chew the end of it, watching her reflectively. 'School out for the summer?'

She shook her head. 'Out for ever. I've been offered a place to read English at London University, if my grades are good enough.'

He sat up. 'Truly? My God, that's terrific.' He grinned at her. 'Your family must be thrilled. Really proud too.'

She returned his smile shyly. 'They seem to be. And I'm quite pleased myself.'

'So what do you plan to do with your eventual degree. Teach?'

She shook her head. 'Journalism, I hope, at least to begin with.' She flushed a little. 'I've always wanted to write, and one day, when I know a little more about life, I might even manage a novel.'

'This calls for a celebration.' Darius got to his feet and strode up the track to where his Land Rover was parked. When he returned, Chloe saw to her astonishment that he was carrying a bottle of champagne and a paper cup.

'No crystal flute, I'm afraid, and it won't be as cold as it should be, but—what the hell?'

She gasped. 'Do you always have champagne in your car?'

'No,' he said, removing the foil. 'This was a farewell present.'

An instinct she'd not been aware she possessed told her that it was from a woman.

She watched with unwilling fascination as he extracted the cork with only the faintest 'pop' then poured the fizzing wine into the cup without spilling a drop.

She said, 'I thought it was supposed to explode out of the bottle and drench everyone around.'

'Only if you've won a Grand Prix.' He handed her the cup, and sat down on the edge of her rock. 'Here's to your first bestseller,' he said, and drank from the bottle.

Chloe hesitated. 'It's kind of you,' she began. 'But I really don't think I should.'

His brows lifted. 'Why not? You've reached an age where all kinds of delights are legally permissible—and this is one of them. It's not drugged, and there's not enough in that cup to render you drunk in charge of a bicycle, so there's no need to be nervous.'

'I'm not,' she denied swiftly.

'Perhaps scared stiff would be more applicable,' he said, his mouth twisting. 'But you're perfectly safe, because I know that if I upset you in any way, I'll have your formidable Aunt Libby to deal with, and she's even scarier.'

She was betrayed into a reluctant giggle.

'That's better,' Darius approved. 'You can't refuse to drink a toast to your own success.'

She lifted the cup to her lips and drank, feeling the bubbles burst against her throat.

'You talk as if it's a foregone conclusion.'

'Maybe because I believe it is,' he said. 'Though I think I'd have put my money on you becoming an actress rather than a writer.'

She took another swallow. 'Why do you say that?'

'I remember how you used to read to my mother,' he said slowly. 'The way you interpreted the words—got inside the characters. You made the books live—gave her real enjoyment.' His smile was reflective. 'She was very fond of you.'

Chloe looked down. 'It's kind of you to say so,' she returned awkwardly. 'I—I liked her too.' She hesitated. 'Actually, I was rather stage-struck for a brief time. But perhaps the readings got me focused on the way stories were constructed and made me realise I'd rather create my own words than interpret what other people had written. If that makes any sense.'

He nodded. 'I gather you still come up to the Hall sometimes to help with the ponies.'

'Yes, but that won't be for much longer.' She couldn't avoid the wistful note in her voice. 'Arthur says Mr Maynard intends to sell them. Yet they're so lovely, and still really strong and healthy. I—I thought he'd have kept them for his own children.'

Darius refilled her paper cup. 'Clearly he has other plans for when that happy time arrives. And Moonrise Lady is going too.'

'Mrs Maynard's mare?' She stared at him. 'But why?'

'Too nervous.'

'She's nothing of the kind.' Chloe's protest was instinctive. 'She has a wonderful temperament.'

'I was talking about the rider,' he said. 'Not the horse. It seems that Penny's not much of a country girl at heart, and much prefers four wheels to four legs.'

'Oh,' she said. 'Well—that's a shame, when Mr Maynard is so keen. My uncle was saying he'll be asked to be Joint Master of the Hunt next season.'

'I've heard that too. Following in a grand old tradition like his father and grandfather before him,' he added, lifting one smooth brown shoulder in a casual shrug.

'Don't you believe in tradition?' It must be the champagne, she thought. She would never have dared question him like this under normal circumstances.

'Fortunately I don't have to,' he said shortly. 'That's Andrew's job. But, for the record, I believe in progress. In doing what needs to be done.'

A sudden flash lit up the sky and he looked up, frowning. 'Which at the moment is to get dressed and out of here,' he added as thunder rumbled ominously in the distance. He emptied the rest of the champagne onto the grass. 'I'll go down by the water, and you use that clump of trees. That should preserve the decencies well enough. But be quick.'

Her hesitation was only momentary. She was just zipping her trousers when, with another crack of lightning, the rain began to fall in thick, heavy drops.

As she made for the track, Darius joined her. 'Get in the Land Rover,' he told her. 'I'll put your bike in the back.'

'But I couldn't ask you...'

'You didn't.' He handed her the keys. 'Now run before you're drenched.'

It was raining in earnest now so it seemed wiser to do as she was told.

She scrambled into the passenger seat, and waited, her heart thumping, while Darius retrieved her cycle and loaded it on board, along with the empty champagne bottle.

'Well, we can't say we weren't warned,' he commented as he started the engine, the rain thudding on the roof. 'But it's a pity our celebration had to end so suddenly. The glories of the English summer.' He glanced at her. 'Not too wet?'

'I'm fine.' She sat up straight, hands folded in her lap. 'It's—very kind of you.'

'What did you imagine?' His swift grin slanted. 'That I'd allow a future Booker prize-winner to risk pneumonia?'

Chloe flushed, and because she couldn't think of a single sensible reply, kept quiet.

When he drew up in front of the Grange he said, 'Here you are, home and dry. And I won't accept the kind invitation to come in for a cup of tea, which I'm sure is trembling on your lips,' he added, as he lifted out her bicycle. 'So let's just say that I'll see you around.'

He paused, then said softly, 'And when your first novel is bought by a publisher, I promise I'll open more champagne and douse you with it—every last inch from your head down to your toes.'

He blew her a kiss, got back in the Land Rover and drove away, leaving her staring after him, lips parted, oblivious to the rain.

Aunt Libby was waiting in the hall. 'My dear child, I knew the weather would turn. You must be soaked to the skin. I'll run you a hot bath.'

'I'm hardly even damp,' Chloe returned. She hesitated. 'Actually, I had a lift home.'

'Well that was good of somebody.' Aunt Libby led the way into the kitchen and busied herself filling the teapot. 'Who was it?'

Chloe tried to sound ultracasual. 'It was Darius Maynard, of all people.'

'Darius?' Aunt Libby placed the lid slowly on the teapot. 'I thought he was supposed to be working on a stud farm in Ireland. Where did you run into him?'

'He came back yesterday,' said Chloe. 'And I met him down at the Willow Pond. He'd gone there for a swim. Like me.'

'I see,' said her aunt in a tone that suggested the revelation was not altogether welcome. She poured tea into two beakers and handed one to her niece. 'I imagine he's back for the Birthday Ball. The invitations are being sent out this week, so I suppose it was inevitable.'

Chloe stared at her. 'You make it sound as if he should have stayed away.'

'Maybe he should, at that.' Mrs Jackson sighed sharply. 'It always seems that whenever Darius is around, there's invariably trouble and some of it, according to the talk in the village, has been serious. Not all his absences, especially the most recent one, have been entirely voluntary.'

Her aunt shook her head, her expression brooding. 'But perhaps it isn't entirely his fault. For one thing, he's so entirely different from his father and older brother, and, for another, being the second son with no actual role to play in the running of the estate can't be a happy situation for him. Maybe it encourages him to be wild. To see how far he can push the boundaries even if it means breaking the law.'

'The law?' Chloe repeated. 'I don't understand.'

'There's no reason why you should,' Aunt Libby said with finality. 'Just keep out of his way, my dear.' She added with faint grimness. 'And being far too attractive for his own good doesn't help either.'

'Well, he doesn't appeal to me,' Chloe said firmly, taking a sip of scalding tea, and hoping it would disguise any lingering hint of wine on her breath.

And just who am I trying to convince here? she asked herself. Aunt Libby—or myself?

Not that it matters. The Maynards belong in a totally different social sphere to the rest of the village, so our paths are unlikely to cross again.

A view confirmed in a few days when the village grapevine spread the word that Darius had left the Hall again, this time for London.

'Always restless, that one,' was Mrs Thursgood's opinion. 'Not happy in the same place for more than a week. Never was. Never will be. Was it a book of six or twelve stamps you were wanting?'

But at least Chloe felt able to relax a little without imagining she might bump into him around the next corner.

And his absence encouraged her to respond to a suggestion from the Hall, conveyed by her uncle over lunch, that as the ponies would be leaving early the following day, she might like to say goodbye to them.

'Well, yes.' She sighed. 'Although I can't believe that Mr Maynard has really sold them, when they've both got years left still. Or that Moonrise Lady is going too.'

'Well at least they're departing for new homes where they'll be loved and wanted, so it makes a kind of sense. And the ponies have been bought together.' Uncle Hal dropped a gentle hand on her shoulder as he rose from the table. 'I'll be passing the Hall presently if you want a lift, but you'll have to walk back.'

Chloe changed quickly, tucking a short-sleeved blue shirt into her jodhpurs. Her uncle dropped her off at the Hall's gates, and she was on her way up the winding drive when a car's horn tooted behind her.

Her heart gave a swift lurch, and she turned apprehensively to see Penny Maynard waving at her from her Alfa Romeo.

'Hop in,' she called. 'It's far too hot to walk.'

As always, she looked devastating, wearing a white skirt topped by a cyclamen-pink blouse, her ash-blonde hair cut into a sleek shoulder-length bob, and her violet eyes fringed by expertly darkened lashes.

She'd always been reed-slender, but now it seemed to Chloe that she was actually thin, and there was an increased definition to her cheekbones and a tautness to her mouth that had not been there before. That made her beautiful face look almost haggard.

'I'm sorry you're losing your playmates,' she remarked as the car sped off. 'After all, you're the one who's really bothered with them. But Andrew has finally accepted that horses are another interest we will never share, so I won't really be shedding any tears.'

There was an odd note in her voice that Chloe could not interpret, and, anyway, this was Sir Gregory's daughter-in-law she was talking to, so she confined her reply to a neutral, 'I suppose not.'

'Prenuptial agreements seem always to be about money,' the older girl went on flatly. 'I think their scope should be broadened, so that everyone knows exactly where they stand. No post-wedding shocks. Don't you agree?'

'I don't know,' Chloe returned with faint bewilderment. 'But you couldn't possibly include everything.' She paused awkwardly. 'Besides, isn't learning about each other all part of the fun of being married?'

'"The fun of being married",' Penny repeated almost musingly. 'Yes, you're quite right. That's what it's all about, of course.' She gave a short laugh. '"Oh, wise young judge".'

She stopped the car at the arch leading into the stable yard to allow Chloe to alight. 'Listen,' she said. 'I want you to know I'm really glad that you cared about the ponies and Moonrise Lady and made a fuss of them, and I'm sorry it couldn't be me. It would at least have been one way of justifying my existence.'

She drove off fast, her tyres scattering gravel, and Chloe watched her departure, astonished and embarrassed at the same time.

What on earth, she wondered, had all that been about?

Penny Maynard was at least six years her senior, and, until now, like most local people, Chloe had admired her at a distance. Certainly, they'd never exchanged more than the minimal formalities if they happened to encounter each other at occasions like the annual village concert or the flower show. And they'd never—ever—been on female chatting terms.

How could we be? Chloe asked herself. When I'm just a schoolgirl and she's a married woman? When she probably knows me only vaguely as the vet's niece? It makes no sense.

In the stable, Arthur Norris, the groom, was tacking up Moonrise Lady. He greeted Chloe with his usual unsmiling nod.

'Ponies are in the first paddock,' he said. 'I've put a few jumps up in the far one, not too high, so you can school this one over them, make sure she minds her manners. Girl she's going to isn't all that experienced.'

'But she's certainly lucky.' Chloe ran a gentle hand down the mare's neck, hearing her whicker softly in response. Penny Maynard, she thought, didn't know what she'd missed.

She extracted a plastic container of apple and carrot pieces from her shoulder bag, and went down to the paddock. The ponies met her at the fence, jostling each other for the pick of the treats, butting her arm and shoulder with eager affection.

She fed them and stroked their noses, whispering that they

should be staying here where they belonged, waiting to take Andrew's children on their backs, but that she'd remember them always. Always.

Then Arthur came down from the yard with Moonrise Lady, and she mounted, blinking back her tears, and rode the little mare into the other paddock.

The jumps were simple ones, and Chloe took her through them with easy grace, then turned, watching Arthur raise the rail a couple of notches on the final one, but keeping it still well within the Lady's capacity.

She rode back to the start, and put the mare at the first low hurdle. Moonrise Lady jumped it perfectly again, continuing to sail effortlessly over the others.

But as they approached the last, Chloe saw out of the corner of her eye a movement over by the paddock gate, and realised they'd been joined by someone else. Momentarily distracted, she allowed herself a quick glance to confirm the identity of the newcomer.

With a gasp, she tried to regain her concentration, but the rhythm of the mare's stride was broken. She took off at an awkward angle, stumbled on landing and sent Chloe flying over her head to hit the grass with a force that left her panting and breathless at the feet of Darius Maynard.

CHAPTER SEVEN

'WELL, I've seen more elegant descents.' Darius squatted beside her. 'Do you think you've broken anything or are you just winded?'

Chloe sat up wincing. 'Just—winded.' *And furious with myself for being such an idiot.*

'Also a little dishevelled,' he said softly.

Following his gaze, Chloe glanced down and saw to her horror that some of the little pearl buttons on her shirt had come undone during her fall, revealing even more of her firm young breasts in their lace-trimmed cups than her bikini bra had done.

'I have no objection, naturally,' Darius added, a quiver of amusement in his voice. 'But you might give poor old Arthur a heart attack.'

So to that fury, she could also add humiliation, she thought as she struggled to refasten her shirt with fingers made clumsy by haste and embarrassment. And in front of him, of all people.

It was a welcome relief when Moonrise Lady came wandering over to drop a soft and questing muzzle on her shoulder and she could bury her flushed face in the mare's neck.

'I'm sorry, darling,' she muttered. 'It was all my fault.'

'She already knows that,' Darius said crisply. He got to his feet, dusting bits of grass from his elegant charcoal pants.

He held out a hand. 'Up you come, my girl, and up you get—back on the Lady; restore her confidence in you by taking her over that last jump again. Properly this time.'

Chloe obeyed mutinously. Not that she had much choice with his hand clasped firmly round hers, pulling her upright.

She wasn't used to being thrown. She felt jolted all over and tomorrow she'd be bruised, and what she really wanted was to burst into tears and go home.

And to say that she'd made a mistake because his unexpected arrival had startled her was no excuse at all.

She lifted herself stiffly into the saddle, took a deep, calming breath then set off as instructed. This time there were no mistakes as Moonrise Lady soared safely and sweetly over the rail and came down as if she was treading on velvet.

As she brought the mare to a halt and made to dismount, Darius reached up, lifting her out of the saddle and depositing her gently on her own two feet, wobbly legs notwithstanding.

'Thank you.' She tried to say it normally but, with his strong hands still grasping her waist, it emerged as a squeak. She stepped back and removed her hat, shaking her hair loose. 'I—I'll see to the Lady.'

'Arthur will do that. I've been instructed to take you up to the house.'

She hesitated, glancing down quickly at the grass stains on her jodhpurs. 'I'm expected at home.'

'My sister-in-law has rung the Grange,' he said. 'Told them you're staying for some tea. Although there won't be much sympathy.' He produced a handkerchief and wiped her cheek, showing her the smear of earth he'd removed. 'And clean you up a little at the same time.'

Colour stormed into her face as she realised what she probably looked like. But she accepted, too, that there was little point in further protest. That she was doomed to appear a grubby urchin beside Penny Maynard's effortless chic.

She hadn't set foot in the house since Lady Maynard's death, but it didn't seem to have changed at all. The hall with its flagged floor, and the family portraits in massive frames on its panelled walls gave its usual cool and shady impression after the blaze of the sun, the only patch of colour provided by a massive silver bowl filled with roses on a long side table.

In the drawing room, Penny was standing by one of the mullioned windows staring fixedly at the garden beyond. As Darius conducted Chloe into the room, she turned, her gaze sharpening.

'Good God, what happened to you?'

'I fell off,' Chloe admitted in a tone of false brightness.

'Off one of my husband's gentle, noble creatures?' Penny's tone was mocking. 'I can hardly believe it.' She walked forward. 'You look as if you've been rolled on and trampled. I'll take you up to my room. Make you look more presentable.' She glanced at Darius. 'Tell Mrs Vernon to give us about twenty minutes before she brings tea, will you?'

As she followed Penny up the stairs, Chloe felt the past few years slip away, turning her back into the nervous fourteen-year-old being conducted to Lady Maynard.

But whereas that bedroom had been massive and stately, filled with valuable antique furniture, Penny's room was in total contrast.

It was all pale colours, and sleek modern lines, down to the low, wide divan bed.

'Andrew offered me free rein with the décor,' Penny tossed carelessly over her shoulder. 'So I took him at his word.'

'It's beautiful,' said Chloe. Beautiful, she thought, but also totally out of place in an old house like this. Nor could she visualise Andrew Maynard's tall, broad-shouldered frame being at ease in all this feminine magnificence. But no doubt he felt his glamorous wife was worth it.

The bathroom was another surprise in ivory and gold, and

more like a beauty salon than a place to wash and clean one's teeth. Or the Hall of Mirrors at Versailles, she thought with a shudder as she caught sight of herself in all her mud-stained glory in one of them. Only her shirt seemed to have escaped relatively unscathed.

'Have a shower if you want,' her hostess invited casually. 'There are loads of towels. And I'll find you something cleaner to wear. I imagine we're about the same size.'

'I don't want to put you to any trouble,' said Chloe, but it was a token protest. Her eyes were already glistening at the sight of the engraved glass cubicle with its power shower.

'You're not.' The denial was instant, but the accompanying smile seemed a little forced. 'Come down when you're ready.'

The cascade of hot water felt like balm on her aching body. When she returned to the bedroom, her jodhpurs had been removed and a pair of jeans with a designer label were waiting for her in their place, together with a short-sleeved white silk blouse, and a hair dryer.

The jeans fitted her like a second skin, and Penny was taller too, so Chloe had to turn up the legs a fraction. But the blouse was a little too large, so at least there was no chance of any more accidents with buttons, she decided, her face warming at the unwelcome memory.

Once dressed again, she sat down rather shyly at the dressing table with its array of scent bottles and cosmetic jars, praying she wouldn't break anything or move a pot of cream out of its designated place, and began to attend to her hair.

At the same time, she found her eyes straying round the room, remembering the enormous four-poster bed in Lady Maynard's bedroom, and the elegant *chaise longue* by the window where the Hall's former mistress had spent so many of her latter days, and wondering what she would have made of all this determined modernity. Or whether Penny would have been gently but firmly dissuaded from its more extreme aspects.

Because Lady Maynard had believed in tradition. Sometimes, when the reading was over and she'd felt well enough, she had talked to Chloe, reminiscing about her girlhood, spent travelling with her parents to various diplomatic posts all over the world, making the past live again with an almost wistful note in her voice.

She'd spoken too of the history of the Hall she'd been compiling over the years, admitting with regretful finality that it would never be finished.

'That will be someone else's task,' she'd said.

I wonder what happened to it? thought Chloe as she switched off the dryer and stood up.

When she got down to the hall, Mrs Vernon was just wheeling the tea trolley into the drawing room.

'Perfect timing,' Darius said, tossing aside the copy of *Horse and Hound* he was reading and getting to his feet as Chloe followed the housekeeper into the room. The green eyes skimmed her, sharpening in undisguised appreciation as they observed how the borrowed jeans moulded her slim hips and the length of her slender legs, before returning almost quizzically to the concealment of the white blouse.

No prizes for guessing what he was thinking, Chloe thought indignantly as the dull colour stole back into her face again. Head high, she stalked over to a chair as far from the sofa he'd been occupying as it was possible to get without actually leaving the room.

I don't want him to look at me like that, she thought passionately. I don't like the way it makes me feel. And I wish he'd stayed up in London, or never come back at all, because I don't like him. Full stop.

Penny was an attentive hostess, offering cucumber sandwiches, scones with jam and cream, and a Madeira cake that managed to be even lighter than Aunt Libby's.

How can she possibly stay so thin with Mrs Denver serving up feasts like this several times a day? Chloe wondered.

Penny chatted too, a rapid flow of words that scarcely demanded an answer, or an intervention from anyone else, telling Chloe how lucky she was to be going to university in London, and what a fun city it could be, talking of theatres, concert halls, galleries and nightclubs.

Or how to be a student on a private income, Chloe thought drily. But she was glad she did not have to sustain the other half of the conversation in any meaningful way. On the surface, it appeared to be a conventional afternoon occasion, but there was a tension in the room that was almost tangible.

And it had to be centred on Darius, she thought, acutely aware of him lounging on the other side of the room, his silk tie loosened, his shirt unbuttoned at the neck as he listened to every word, a half-smile playing round his lips. She remembered what Aunt Libby had said about him. Someone who pushed even the law to its limits.

She found herself wondering exactly what he had done, and why he'd been sent away.

But that was forbidden territory, and she was glad to be able to get up, murmuring that she must be going, thanking Penny for her delicious tea, but swiftly declining her offer of a lift, on the grounds that the walk back to the Grange would do her good.

'Stop me stiffening up too much,' she added.

'But you must take this with you. Your family's invitation to the Birthday Ball.' Her hostess handed her a square white envelope, addressed, Chloe saw, not just to her aunt and uncle, but, for the first time ever, to herself as well.

She held it awkwardly, feeling a bit like Cinderella. 'Thank you. I—I must pop back to the stables before I

leave—pick up my bag.' She forced a smile. 'So thanks
again—and goodbye.'

Hurrying as best she could, she'd reached the archway into
the yard when Darius caught up with her.

She said tautly, staring straight ahead of her, 'You really
don't need to see me off the premises. I know my way.'

'I'm sure you do.' He followed her into the stable, leaning
against the door as he watched her tuck the invitation into
her bag. Apart from the sounds of Moonrise Lady happily
chomping on some hay in her stall and the cooing of a pigeon
in the rafters, it was very quiet. Even, she realised, isolated,
with Arthur nowhere to be seen.

He went on, 'But I also have something to give you.'

He took a small bottle of tablets from his pocket, grinning
as her eyes widened. 'And it's not some weird drug to render
you helpless and at my mercy, either. It's just arnica for the
bruises. I'm sure your uncle has plenty, but consider it a pre-
caution.'

Darius Maynard, Chloe thought bitterly as she accepted
the bottle with a muttered word of thanks, and pushed it into
her bag, king of the disarming gesture.

He added, 'And I'll drive you home.'

'No!' The refusal was too quick and too sharp, and she
saw his brows lift mockingly.

'Chloe, my sweet,' he said softly. 'What must I do to prove
that you can trust me?'

'Nothing,' she said raggedly. 'I simply don't want it to be
necessary.' She swallowed. 'I know it's all a big joke to you,
but it's one I don't happen to share.' She spread her hands
almost helplessly. 'So, why can't you just understand that—
and leave me alone?'

'Because this is not a joke,' he said with sudden harshness.
'Which is something that you in turn are failing to understand.'

He stepped forward, and his hands grasped her shoulders, pulling her towards him.

The breath caught in her throat. She lifted her hands, placing them flat against his chest in a hurried attempt to keep him away from her. Because she had to do something—*something*—to stop him. Before it was too late…

Then he bent his head and his lips took hers with a quiet and almost frightening precision, exploring its soft contours as if her mouth was some unknown territory he was learning by heart, and she knew, as if he had spoken the words aloud, that it was already too late. And perhaps always had been.

One hand moved down and grasped her hip, urging her body into an even more intimate proximity with his. His other hand also abandoned her shoulder to gently stroke the vulnerable line of her throat, and the delicate whorls of her ear before moving to the nape of her neck to let his fingers twine in the soft, dark fall of her hair.

Her own fingers were curling into fists, as they clutched the crisp front of his snowy shirt, holding him as if she was drowning, or her shaking legs would suddenly hold her upright no longer.

His lips coaxed hers apart to allow him to penetrate her mouth's inner sweetness and she felt the satin glide of his tongue teasing hers, playing with its tip in the kind of sensuous demand she'd never experienced before, and she felt the shock of it whisper through her body, startling her innocence with the promise of her own sexuality. Making it impossible for her to deny him the response he sought. Or even wish to…

His kiss deepened instantly, passionately, sending sharp tendrils of sensation quivering along her nerve endings. Her hands slid up to his shoulders, then fastened round his neck, the brush of his hair like silk against her fingers.

And the little voice in her head protesting that this was all wrong, that it was dangerous—it was madness and she should stop it now—*now*—faded to a whisper and then to silence.

They stood, mouths and bodies locked together. For the first time, Chloe felt her clothing as a barrier. She was aware that her breasts seemed to be blooming—swelling against the confines of her bra, pressing against the hard muscularity of his chest, and she wanted to be rid of it. Rid of everything.

As if in answer to some unspoken plea, Darius slid his hand from her hip to her waist, then upwards to cup one soft mound in his palm, while the ball of his thumb moved gently against the delicate rosy peak in deliberate, provocative arousal. She gasped against his mouth, a small choked sound that was almost a moan, as she felt the sudden rush of scalding heat between her thighs.

She heard him groan something that might have been her name, then his caressing hand stilled. He took his lips very slowly from hers and began to kiss her temples, her closed eyes, the line of her cheekbones, and, with great care, the corners of her mouth, just brushing her skin as softly as the wing of a butterfly.

She raised leaden lids and looked up at him, seeing a glitter in the green eyes that scared and excited her at the same time.

When he spoke, his voice was husky, almost slurred. He said, 'No—not here, my sweet one. Not—like this.'

He drew her close and held her for a long moment, his arms almost fierce, his face buried in her hair. Then he straightened, putting her away from him, looking down at her with faint ruefulness.

He said quietly, 'And now I really am going to take you home.'

There were tears on her face as she sat staring unseeingly into the darkness and Chloe wiped them away with her knuckles in a gesture that was almost childish. But every haunting memory of that time, seven years before, was conspiring to remind her that she had indeed been hardly more than a child just emerging into womanhood.

And I indulged myself with a child's dreams, she thought bitterly. Ignored the warnings from people who'd known him so much longer and so much better than I had and who, therefore, had no illusions about him. Told myself they were simply prejudiced, making unfair comparisons with Andrew, who never put a foot wrong.

Darius asked me to trust him, and for a while I did, although I had no cause—no reason to do so. Because I was young and stupid, I let his touch, his kisses tempt me to forget what I really wanted from life. Even to fool myself, for a brief time, that he might be the one—the other half of myself.

And, oh, God, he made it so easy for me. So terribly, heart-breakingly easy.

She shivered suddenly, wrapping her arms round her body.

I mustn't use emotive words like that, she told herself. My heart did not break. It didn't even develop a hairline crack, because Darius was just a diversion. Fate's way of teaching me to distinguish the substance from the shadow. A painful but necessary lesson.

And I won't make the same mistake again.

But she soon found that time hadn't totally done its healing work, and the pain still existed, twisting inside her as she remembered driving back to the Grange with him, her body hot and aching, her hands clasped in her lap to hide the fact that they were trembling.

When she asked him in a small, hoarse voice to drop her at the end of the lane, he made no protest, but she saw his mouth tighten wryly.

As she fumbled her seat belt he leaned across and released

it for her, running a finger gently down the curve of her cheek. He said, 'I'll be in touch,' and drove off.

'So, tea at the Hall,' said Aunt Libby. 'Did you have a nice time?'

Chloe met her enquiring gaze with as much composure as she could manage. 'Yes, Mrs Maynard was very kind. I must wash and iron the clothes she lent me and return them.' She handed over the big square envelope. 'And she sent you this.'

Her aunt's brows rose as she extracted the card and read it. 'You've also been invited, I see. I imagine you won't want to go.'

'Why not?'

'Because I recall you shuddering away from the idea not that long ago, describing the Ball as a bunch of old fogeys dancing the St Bernard's waltz,' Aunt Libby returned calmly.

Chloe flushed. 'Well, yes, I probably did—then.'

'But something's happened to change your mind?' Mrs Jackson's eyes were shrewd.

'It's probably my only opportunity to go.' She forced a smile. 'See if I was right about it. Once I'm at university, I'm going to have to find vacation work, so I won't be around so much.'

'No,' Aunt Libby said thoughtfully. 'There is that.' She was silent for a moment, then gave a brief sigh. 'Then I'll accept for the three of us. You'll need a dress, of course.'

'There's a hire place in East Ledwick,' Chloe said quickly. 'Or I can try the charity shops. It needn't cost much.'

'Clearly you have it all worked out.' Her aunt's tone was dry. 'We'll drive over later this week. See what's available.'

It was not a prolonged search. The woman who ran the dress hire ran a brisk eye over Chloe and nodded in approval. 'Lovely slim figure and slightly high-waisted too. I think I have the perfect thing.'

She disappeared to the back of the shop and returned with a swathe of filmy fabric in white, shot with the glimmer of silver, draped over her arm.

'I'm told this has been inspired by the new *Pride and Prejudice* film due out in the autumn,' she announced. 'Whatever, I think it's delightful.'

And when Chloe looked at herself in the mirror, she could only agree. It was a slender column of a dress, short-sleeved, the ankle-length skirt falling straight from a low-cut bodice which permitted an enticing but demure glimpse of the first swell of her breasts.

'Elizabeth Bennet to the life.' The manageress smiled at her, then turned to Aunt Libby. 'Is there a Mr Darcy waiting to dance with her?'

'Absolutely not.' Mrs Jackson spoke with a certain crispness. 'As such men only exist in the pages of books. But the dress is certainly charming, and I doubt whether anything else will have the same appeal, so we'll take it.'

A shoe shop in the High Street provided the final touch of an inexpensive pair of silver ballerina pumps, and Chloe accomplished the journey home in a mood of quiet elation, barely noticing that Aunt Libby was equally silent.

They were almost at the Grange when her aunt said abruptly, 'Next time Ian calls, why don't you ask him if he can get back for the weekend of the dance? I'm sure if we explain the circumstances, Mrs Maynard will give us an extra invitation.'

Chloe looked at her, startled. 'But it wouldn't be any use. The programme is an ongoing thing. He doesn't have weekends off.'

'Well there would be no harm in trying.' Aunt Libby shot her a swift glance. 'That's if you want him to go with you, of course.'

'Well, naturally I do.' Chloe recognised the defensive note in her voice. 'In fact, I'll ring him this evening.'

However, 'Not a cat's chance, I'm afraid,' Ian told her glumly. 'The team's one short as it is. Craig's off with shingles.'

'It can't be helped.' Chloe tried to sound consoling. 'It was just an idea.'

But as she hung up, she caught a glimpse of herself in the mirror above the hall table and knew, with shame, that her eyes were much too bright for real disappointment.

Over breakfast the next day, she said casually, 'I'd better iron Mrs Maynard's clothes and return them. I'd almost forgotten.'

'I hadn't,' said her aunt, composedly buttering a slice of toast. 'I laundered them, and got your uncle to drop them off at the Hall a couple of days ago.'

'Oh.' Chloe stared down at her plate, hiding her chagrin. 'I didn't mean you to go to all that trouble.'

'Nothing of the kind,' said Aunt Libby. 'It was my pleasure.'

And there, seething, Chloe had to allow the matter to rest.

But now, looking back down the years, she realised that her aunt had only been trying to be wise for her. To steer her gently away from the first real danger of her young life.

She could see it, she thought. Why couldn't I?

Except, of course, that it was already too late, she admitted, shivering. Because the damage was done, leaving her to face its bitter consequences and, somehow, learn to endure them.

CHAPTER EIGHT

BY THE night at the ball, Chloe had been so nervous she almost wished she'd developed shingles herself.

But the dress had looked even better than it had in the shop, and she'd caught back her newly washed tumble of dark curls, securing them away from her face with two pretty silver combs.

'You look lovely, my dear,' Uncle Hal greeted her as she came downstairs. 'Isn't she a picture, Libby? The belle of the ball in person.'

Her aunt, elegant in a plain black dress topped by a hip-length sequinned jacket, smiled affectionately and nodded, and if she still had concerns, she kept them well hidden.

The ballroom at the Hall was at the rear of the house, and was approached through a large conservatory where Sir Gregory waited to receive his guests, with Andrew Maynard beside him, the formality of evening clothes emphasising the rigidity of his demeanour, and making him look more like a soldier on parade than a man at the start of a pleasant social occasion.

But his tension appeared to be shared. Penny stood next to him, ravishing in a deep fuchsia-pink sheath, but her face under her immaculately piled-up hair was taut, and her smile seemed as if it had been painted on.

While of Darius, there was no sign.

As Chloe paused in front of Penny to say a shy, 'Good evening,' the older girl gave a slight nod, then turned calling 'Laurence.'

A tall, fair young man detached himself from a nearby group and came towards them.

'Yes, Mrs Maynard?'

'This is Chloe Benson, our local vet's daughter,' Penny drawled. 'It's her first Birthday Ball, so make sure she meets a few people of her own age, please.'

Laurence did not appear overjoyed to have been appointed resident babysitter, and Chloe, smarting at Penny's casual attitude, shared his reservations in full. It was far from being the introduction to the ball that she'd hoped for. Which proved only how silly it was possible to be, she thought as she followed him reluctantly.

And her misgivings seemed entirely justified as one of the girls in the group they were approaching looked at her dress and said in a stage whisper, 'I thought this was a dance, not a fancy dress parade,' setting off a faint ripple of amusement.

'Meet Chloe Benson,' Laurence announced. 'Apparently she's a local.'

'Really?' One of the other girls raised her eyebrows. 'I don't remember you at St Faiths?' She was referring to the expensive girls' day school on the other side of East Ledwick, and Chloe shook her head.

'I went to Freemont High School.'

'Oh,' said the other. 'Oh, I see. Well, I suppose that would explain it.'

'Did you think tonight was fancy dress?' The original speaker was back on the attack, looking her over.

Flushing, Chloe lifted her chin. 'No,' she returned. 'I'm simply wearing a dress I fancied.' And allowed her own appraising glance to suggest that scarlet taffeta was not the wisest choice for someone at least a stone overweight.

'And why wouldn't you?' A brown-haired girl with mischievous hazel eyes came forward. 'I'm Fran Harper,' she said. 'And, for the record, I think you look fabulous. Classic.' She paused. 'There's some great punch on offer in the dining room. Let's find you some and get acquainted.'

As they walked away together, she added in an undertone, 'Don't let Judy or Mandy get to you. They both fancy Laurence for some unknown reason, and you represent instant threat.'

'Not really,' Chloe told her ruefully. 'We were simply foisted on each other by Mrs Maynard. She probably thought she was being kind.'

'Good God,' said Fran. 'She's never struck me as the charitable sort. A lady with axes of her own to grind, I'd have said.'

She ladled punch into two small glass cups, and handed one to Chloe.

'To kindness, however unlikely it may be,' she announced, and drank.

Chloe sipped with rather more caution, feeling the warmth curl in her throat as she tried to glance round the room without making it too obvious that she was looking for someone.

But it was patently evident that Darius was still not around and she found herself stifling a pang of disappointment.

Ludicrous, she told herself firmly, and high time that she came to her senses and started to enjoy the evening simply for what it was rather than letting herself indulge in dangerous imaginings.

Besides, her view of the room was soon restricted as others came to join them, and she found herself in the middle of a cheerful group of people her own age or slightly older, most of whom had already embarked on their university careers, and appeared genuinely interested in her own plans.

Before too long, they'd all adjourned to the ballroom, and Chloe was immediately out on the floor, dancing firstly with

Fran's brother Bas, in his second year at Cambridge, followed by a whole series of other boys.

She was laughingly protesting that she needed a rest when she felt an odd tingle of awareness shiver down her spine and, looking over the shoulder of a stocky brown-haired boy with freckles, saw Darius on the other side of the floor partnering a tall grey-haired woman in emerald-green.

Her heart leapt so fiercely, she was ashamed. Nor was she proud, either, to be thankful that she too was dancing and not occupying one of the chairs at the side of the room in solitary splendour, dumped there by Laurence and co. Just in case he happened to notice.

But she must never forget either that, if circumstances had allowed, she'd have been here tonight with Ian, and happy to be so. That was the most important thing. So how could she possibly be even glancing in any other direction—and especially one so patently impossible?

I need to stop all this, she told herself with a kind of desperation. I need to stop it right now, before I make an utter fool of myself. And she gave Craig with the freckles the kind of smile that made his pleasant face light up in response.

But good intentions notwithstanding, she could probably have given a photo-fit description of every woman Darius had danced with throughout the evening. As for herself, there was no indication that he was even aware of her presence.

It was almost a relief when a halt was called for supper. This, served in the dining room, was on traditional lines, with large joints of ham and beef for carving, platters of salmon mayonnaise, coronation chicken, lobster patties, mushroom and asparagus tartlets, a huge array of salads, cheeses and baskets of crusty bread. Also on offer were bowls of rich chocolate mousse, tall frosted glasses of syllabub, and great dishes piled with strawberries accompanied by clotted cream.

Chloe wished that she wasn't feeling so tense, and could have done the spread rather more justice.

And on the heels of supper, came the birthday toast, proposed with due formality by Sir Gregory, flanked by both his sons, with Penny Maynard standing, slender as a willow wand but with all the rigidity of a steel rod at her husband's side, her faint smile looking as if it had been painted on.

'In asking you to pay this tribute to my great-grandmother Lavinia,' he announced, his deep voice booming over the crowded room, 'I would also like to include all the other wives since who have done such honour to the Maynard name as chatelaines here. Not forgetting my daughter-in-law Penelope,' he added, turning towards her. 'Who, I have no doubt, will bring her own charm and distinction to this role.'

He raised his champagne glass. 'My lord, ladies and gentlemen, I give you—the Maynard ladies.'

'The Maynard ladies,' was echoed smilingly round the room. Chloe, about to sip, found for some reason that her eyes were drawn to Penny Maynard who had blushed to the colour of a peony as Sir Gregory spoke. But as Chloe watched, the hectic flush faded, leaving her pale as a ghost apart from the artificial pink curve of her mouth and the vivid, over-bright eyes.

My God, Chloe thought in horror. She's going to faint.

There was little she could do from the back of the room, but she took an instinctive step forward just the same in time to see Penny turn and walk slowly and steadily away, leaving the three men standing together, like an awkwardly posed study in black-and-white.

The moment of crisis, if that was what it had been, seemed to have passed, but it left Chloe feeling curiously uneasy, just the same.

She was almost glad when the dancing resumed again, even though the knowledge that her aunt and uncle had no intention of staying on into the small hours made her feel far more like Cinderella than Elizabeth Bennet. She would just enjoy whatever time she had left, she told herself.

She was recovering her breath and drinking some lime and soda when she saw Laurence, of all people, making his way towards her with an ingratiating smile.

'Come on, princess,' he said softly as he reached her. 'I think it's time we got it together, don't you?'

'Afraid not, old boy.' The speaker, a tall red-haired young man appeared from nowhere. 'She's promised to me.

'And I have a definite feeling,' he went on, steering Chloe expertly towards the French windows which had been opened onto the terrace. 'That we should sit this one out.'

Chloe tried to pull away in swift alarm. 'I really don't think so.'

'Trust me, sweetheart.' Clasping her firmly, he whirled her down to the far end of the terrace in some kind of old-fashioned waltz that had nothing to do with the music being played. 'They don't call me Honest Jack Prendergast for nothing.'

'I wasn't aware they called you anything at all,' Chloe snapped, still trying to free herself.

'Well why don't you check with a mutual friend?' he said soothingly, and swung her round as a dark figure emerged from the shadows. 'Here she is, mate, delivered as per request, feathers a little ruffled, but I'm sure you can deal with that.' He gave a broad grin. 'Bless you my children.' And he strode back up the terrace leaving Chloe looking up at Darius.

'Sorry about the cloak and dagger stuff,' he said lightly. 'But every time I tried to get over to you, I was intercepted for one reason or another. An elliptical approach seemed better, so I enlisted Jack's assistance and took a different route.'

'I can't imagine why,' said Chloe, unsure whether she was

breathless from the waltz or the shocked clamour of her own heartbeat.

'And you say you're going to be a writer?' he queried softly. 'You'll have to use your imagination better than that, Miss Benson.' His hands went round her waist, drawing her slowly and inexorably towards him so that they melded into the shadows.

And even though a small warning voice in her head was telling her to release herself from his grasp and run back to where there were lights and people and safety, in reality her lips were already parting, longing for his kiss.

His mouth was warm and almost frighteningly gentle as it took hers but his lightest touch was enough to send every sense, each nerve ending in her untutored body into quivering, aching response. Chloe pressed herself against him, her arms twining round his neck as she gave herself up to the sweet delirium of the moment.

She felt his clasp tighten around her to the point of ruthlessness, as his kiss deepened, and his tongue invaded her mouth in frankly sensual demand and clung to him with all the passion of her newly awakened flesh.

When Darius raised his head, his breathing was ragged. 'God, sweetheart.' His voice was unsteady. 'Have you any idea what you're doing to me?'

'Yes.' The word was scarcely more than a breath. How could she not know, she thought, when every waking and sleeping moment since their last meeting had burned with the memory of him? Of their last encounter...

No—not here. Not like this...

His words, heavy with a desire that was now overwhelming her with the need for surcease. The necessity to know— everything.

Her fingertips wonderingly explored the planes and contours of his face, stroking the high cheekbones and the hard

line of his jaw. She took his hand and kissed it, then pressed
it to the delicate mound of her breast and its taut, excited nipple, hearing him groan softly as he began to caress her, his
fingers pushing aside the concealing fabric of her dress.

But in that same moment, they heard the sudden sound
of voices and laughter from the other end of the terrace, and
knew they had company.

'We can't stay here,' Darius said, his tone oddly harsh. 'I
have to be alone with you. Will you go with me?'

She nodded, the movement little more than a nervous jerk
of the head as she realised exactly what her consent entailed.
What she was deliberately inviting.

He took her hand, steering her quickly round the corner
of the terrace and down some stone steps onto the wide grav-
elled path that traversed the house until they came to a side
door.

Inside was a flagged passage and, at its end, a flight of
wooden stairs leading up to a swing door and beyond it a
dimly lit, thickly carpeted corridor that she had never seen
on any of her previous visits, although instinct told her what
their ultimate destination would be.

Halfway along, Darius paused and opened another door,
ushering her inside. It was his bedroom, as she'd known it
would be, even if the lamp left alight on the night table had
not revealed as much.

But a first glance told her that it was far from the kind
of room she'd have expected. For one thing, it wasn't very
large and the furnishings, including the three-quarter-size
bed under its plain green quilt, were fairly sparse, consisting
of a single wardrobe in some dark wood, a matching chest of
drawers with a mirror, and a small armchair.

There were no pictures on the plain walls or ornaments on
any of the surfaces, and if it hadn't been for the hairbrushes
and small group of toiletries on the dressing chest, the dis-

carded jeans and shirt tossed over the chair, the small pile of books on the night table and the neat pile of luggage in one corner, she'd have believed it was simply a spare room, furnished as an afterthought and only used when the house was full.

A temporary place, she thought, suddenly bewildered, for someone who was just passing through, but surely not for a son of the house?

Then Darius, his dinner jacket and black tie discarded, took her in his arms and all thought surrendered helplessly to sensation as he lifted her and carried her to the bed, kicking off his shoes and dark silk socks before joining her.

For a while, they lay wrapped in each other's arms, kissing slowly and languorously, then Darius began to touch her, his hands moving without haste, exploring the slender lines of her body through the thin layers of material that still hid her, before unfastening the small row of buttons at the back of the bodice and slipping it off her shoulders so that his fingers and his lips could enjoy her bared breasts, stroking and suckling them with sensuous tenderness.

Chloe, eyes closed, let her head fall back on the pillow, a faint moan escaping her throat as she experienced the heavenly torment of this new delight, her nipples hardening to sensitised peaks under the subtle play of his tongue.

'Oh, God, my sweet.' His voice was husky, and she discovered the erotic charge of tasting her scent on his mouth as it returned to hers, while his sure hand released the remaining buttons, so that he could slide down her dress and remove it with infinite care, leaving her with her tiny white lace briefs as her only covering.

She gave a little murmur compounded of pleasure and shyness, her unpractised hands trying desperately to deal with the studs on his dress shirt so that she could feel his naked skin against her own. And Darius helped her, almost negligently stripping the crisp linen away from his body and dropping it to the floor beside the bed, then drawing her against him so that his smooth tanned chest grazed her rounded softness.

She lifted herself, pressing against him in her need to be closer yet, some instinct she'd not known she possessed until that moment telling her there was only one path to the fulfilment of her desire. That he had to be part of her, one flesh with her.

He whispered her name against her mouth, then kissed her with ascending passion and yearning, his hands sliding the length of her spine and pushing away the few inches of lace in order to caress the silken swell of her buttocks. A heartbeat later and the lace was gone, leaving her naked in his arms

Darius lifted himself onto an elbow and looked down at her, his eyes shadowed as he gazed at the flushed ivory of her body, the deep rose of her aroused nipples, the concavity of her belly, and the soft dark smudge at the joining of her thighs.

He said in a voice she hardly recognised, 'Do you know how lovely you are? How totally adorable? My glorious, radiant girl.'

His hand swooped over the curve of her hip, then trailed downwards with deliberate purpose combined with a tantalising lack of haste.

Chloe gasped helplessly, as her body responded with a scalding rush of betraying heat to this new and devastating promise and the certainty of where it must lead.

Her own fingers gripped the broad muscular strength of his shoulders, then feathered down over his ribcage and taut abdomen to the waistband of his pants, fumbling with the fastening and tugging down the zip, feeling the hot, steel-like hardness of him through the silk shorts beneath.

Darius freed himself swiftly from the enveloping fabric and kicked it away, sending his shorts after it, then pulling her to him, letting her feel the ramrod urgency of him between her bare thighs.

She made some small incoherent sound and opened herself to him. His mouth took hers and she felt the silken play of his tongue mirroring the first heart-stopping glide of his fingertips as they moved on her with a lingering and exquisite finesse she'd never dreamed could exist.

But no dream had ever taken her this far, overwhelming her in mind, body and soul, making her ache, burn and melt. Turning her innocence in a few brief moments to a distant and unregretted memory.

And if in some dazed corner of her mind, she realised this was because she was in the hands of a master in the art of seduction, she did not attempt to resist because she also knew that she could not, even if she wanted to.

He found her woman's tiny sensitive mound among the heated satin folds of flesh and stroked it softly and sweetly, arousing it to a throbbing peak of anticipation. Yet, all the same, when his exploration of her deepened to a first gentle penetration, she could not help flinching a little as it occurred to her what the reality of a full physical consummation would mean.

Darius stopped instantly. 'I'm hurting you?'

She found a voice from somewhere. 'No. At least… It's just that I've never…'

Her voice tailed away in embarrassment, and she waited for him to take her in his arms and offer reassurance. Tell her that he would make her transition into womanhood beautiful for her.

Instead, there was an odd silence.

Then, as she was trying to pluck up the courage to look at him, he said very quietly, 'Of course. How could I possibly not realise? Hell, how blind and selfish is it possible to be?'

She did stare at him then, her eyes widening endlessly in

bewilderment and a kind of fear as she heard the detached weariness in his voice.

She said, faltering again, 'Is something wrong?'

'Just about everything, I'd say.' He was moving to the edge of the bed, reaching for his clothes, presenting her with the implacable view of his naked back. 'But principally—that I haven't the least right in the world to make this kind of demand of you. And thank God you made me see it before too much harm was done.'

'I don't understand.' Her voice shook. 'I thought you wanted me.'

'Who wouldn't, my sweet?' His drawl made the words no easier to hear. 'As I said earlier you are—very lovely—and frantically desirable. But that is no justification for stealing your virginity in what would probably be a pretty one-sided transaction.'

'Then why did you bring me here?'

He told her why in a brief explicit crudity that brought the colour storming into her face, and impelled her to cover herself with her hands. Not that he was even glancing in her direction.

'I suggest you also get dressed,' he went on. 'I'd leave you in privacy, but you're going to need help with those damned buttons.'

Through the tightness in her throat, she said, 'I managed at home, thank you.'

'Then I'll go. It would naturally be better if we don't arrive downstairs together.' His tone was brisk, almost impersonal. 'If you turn right out of here, then left at the end of the corridor, you'll come out in the Long Gallery. You'll remember your way from there.' He went to the door, carrying his jacket and tie, then turned. In the lamplight, his face was a stranger's—bleak, even haggard.

He said, 'This should never have started, and I can only

ask you to forgive me, and believe me when I tell you that parting now is totally for the best. One day, I hope you'll understand.'

No, Chloe thought, as the door closed softly behind him. I never will.

Not as long as I live.

For the moment, she felt numb, but soon there would be the pain of humiliation and the sheer agony of regret, and she could only pray she'd be safely back at Axford Grange before they kicked in.

Her hands were trembling so much that getting back into her dress was a nightmare, but even the struggle with the buttons was infinitely better than having to submit to his touch again.

Now all she had to do was live with the knowledge that she'd naively offered everything of herself that she had to give to Darius Maynard and been rejected, presumably because her confession of total inexperience had suddenly made her less appealing.

But surely he must have known I'd never been with a man before? she thought, forcing herself to use his brush to restore her hair to some kind of order. Or had he listed me as one of the local tarts? The thought made her shudder.

Her bag was down in the ballroom, so she had no lipstick to return some colour to her white face. One of her combs was missing too, and she had to search for it in the bed, but at last she was fit to be seen again.

As she descended the staircase, Penny Maynard appeared. 'Oh, there you are at last. Your aunt and uncle have been looking for you. I think they're ready to leave.'

'Thank you. I'm sorry I kept them waiting.' Chloe forced a smile. 'I think I had too much punch earlier, so I needed a few quiet moments.'

Penny shrugged. 'It happens,' she said. 'It was one of

Darius's concoctions and they're always lethal. You've probably had a lucky escape.'

'Yes.' Chloe kept her smile, although it felt as if it had been nailed to her mouth. 'I think I probably have.'

And she walked quietly away to find the people who loved her and go home with them, so she could break her heart in secrecy and peace.

CHAPTER NINE

CHLOE stirred awkwardly on the window seat. She was cold and cramped, but that did not explain or justify the tears running down her face. Remembering the events of seven years before had hardly been an exorcism of her personal demons, after all, but more the deliberate opening of an old and still-vicious wound.

She had cried for what remained of the night of the Birthday Ball too, deep racking sobs that threatened to tear her apart. Earlier, she'd explained her disappearance at the dance to her aunt and uncle by saying that she'd felt unwell after supper, and thought she'd eaten something which had disagreed with her.

'You look like a little ghost.' Aunt Libby had viewed her, frowning anxiously. 'Don't think about getting up tomorrow. Sleep as long as you want.'

And, in the end, when there were no tears left, she'd done exactly that. She'd eventually woken around midday, had a bath and dressed in jeans and a tee shirt, but the face that looked back at her from the mirror as she brushed her hair was still wan with deep shadows under the eyes.

Sooner or later, she would have to face Darius again, probably in public, she told herself, and right now she didn't see how that could ever be possible.

She had to practise a few cheerful expressions before she went downstairs.

When she went into the kitchen Uncle Hal had returned for lunch, and he and Aunt Libby were standing by the window, their faces grave, having a low-voiced conversation which ceased abruptly when Chloe entered.

She checked. 'I'm sorry. Is this something private?'

'No. Oh, no.' Aunt Libby's distress was evident. 'It's common knowledge by now, I don't doubt, in every sordid detail. Mrs Thursgood will have seen to that.'

Chloe felt a sudden inexplicable chill. 'Why, what's happened?' *Oh, God did someone see me leaving his bedroom? Has something been said?*

'There's serious trouble at the Hall,' Uncle Hal said abruptly. 'Mrs Maynard—Penny—has left Andrew and run off with his worthless brother. It seems they were found together in his bedroom at some unearthly hour this morning in what's known as "compromising circumstances."' He pronounced the words with distaste. 'It's anyone's guess how long it's been going on.

'There was a terrible scene apparently,' he went on. 'Shouting, hysterics, and even blows exchanged. In the end Sir Gregory told Darius to go and never come back. And he has gone, taking her with him. Cleared out, the pair of them, lock, stock and barrel. And no-one knows where they've gone.'

There was a peculiar roaring in Chloe's ears, and she felt as if she was looking at her aunt and uncle down a long tunnel.

She thought, I must not—I cannot—faint...

Aunt Libby was speaking. 'Mind you, it was pretty obvious last night that all wasn't well. I don't think she and Andrew even had a duty dance together. But all marriages go through rough times, at one time or another.' She sighed.

'Such a good-looking couple, too. It seems so sad. And so awful for Sir Gregory, who values his privacy, to have his family's dirty linen washed in public like this.'

She shook her head. 'I suppose there'll be a divorce.'

'Inevitable, I'd say,' her husband agreed.

Chloe swallowed. 'How—how did you get to know all this?' she asked, astonished that her voice could sound so normal.

'Mrs Thursgood's niece Tracey was helping with the clearing up after the dance,' said her uncle. 'As soon as the row began, they were all out in the hall listening, and, of course, they heard everything. Especially Sir Gregory bellowing at Darius that he didn't have a single shred of decency in his entire body and that if he didn't get out, he'd throw him out with his own hands. And shortly afterwards, Darius and Penny came down with their cases, got into his car and drove away. Well, he's always been the rotten apple in the Maynard barrel with his womanising and other antics. And I dare say a lot of people will be saying "good riddance".'

To bad rubbish. Wasn't that how the quotation ended? Chloe asked herself. And how could she argue with it when Darius, knowing full well that he was committed to someone else, however illicitly, had deliberately set out to seduce her?

But why? she asked herself, feeling genuinely sick to her stomach as she thought of him entwined with Penny on the same bed where he'd been making love to her only a few hours previously. How many women could he possibly want at a time?

She supposed she should be thankful that what passed for his conscience had spared her when she told him she was a virgin. Maybe there was a lingering shred of decency in him after all.

My glorious, radiant girl. The remembered words made her shiver, her throat muscles tightening convulsively. Everything he'd said and done meant nothing. It had all been simply a means to an indecent end. The gratification of a spare hour. If not her, then someone else. But someone with experience, not an innocent idiot. That was what had stopped him, she told herself.

'It's time we ate.' Aunt Libby was bustling around, placing a bowl of salad on the table and cutting slices of a bacon-and-egg pie.

And Chloe had to eat. Had to sit at the table and listen to all the continued conjecture and force down the food, one small mouthful at a time.

'I think Penny Maynard must have taken leave of her senses,' said Aunt Libby. 'How could she not be happy with a decent man like Andrew? And what kind of life is she expecting with that—fly-by-night?'

But she wasn't happy, thought Chloe. Not ever. How could anyone not see that? She was always tense—on edge. So brittle you expected her to snap.

Uncle Hal shrugged. 'Maybe it was just a fling and she never intended it to be found out, only they got careless.' He shook his head. 'Whatever, they're stuck with each other now.'

But were they? Chloe wondered now, uncurling herself from the window seat and standing up. Why wasn't Penny there at the Hall with Darius? Was it all over between them, or had Sir Gregory's forgiveness only extended to his own flesh and blood, permitting no more than the return of the prodigal?

And what does it matter anyway? she asked herself silently as she dried her face, wiped her eyes, blew her nose and got back into bed. It was all a long time ago, and we are different people with different lives now. I know what my future will be and who I'll spend it with. Probably Darius does too, she added, thumping the pillow, and if Lindsay Watson turns out to be his choice, at least his father should approve.

It took her a while to fall asleep, and when she finally did so, she found herself tormented with the kind of dreams that hadn't troubled her for a long time. Dreams that she was imprisoned by silken cords, unable to resist, while a man's hands and mouth explored her body with voluptuous sensuality.

And when she woke, her skin was slick with sweat and her entire self was one shivering ache of yearning.

While the words *my glorious, radiant girl* were, for reasons she did not dare examine too closely, still churning somewhere in her brain.

And Memory Lane, she told herself grimly, is now permanently out of bounds.

'So they're having another of their Birthday Balls,' said Mrs Thursgood, with a sniff. 'Asking for trouble, I'd say. Who's going to be running off with someone they shouldn't from this one, I wonder?'

Chloe, her face wooden, placed her letter on the scales. 'Postage to France, please,' she said.

'France is it?' Mrs Thursgood adjusted her glasses and peered at the electronic reading. 'Getting a job over there, are you?'

'No,' said Chloe. 'I have a friend who's working on the Riviera.'

If it's any of your business, you nosy old bat, she added silently. But I'd rather be interrogated about Tanya than talk about the Birthday Ball.

But Mrs Thursgood was not to be deterred. 'Darius Maynard's been away in London for a good while. It's a wonder his father can spare him. But he's always here and there, that one. Probably keeps a lady friend up there out of the way.'

Chloe, conscious of a growing and interested queue behind her, bit her lip until she tasted blood and forced herself to concentrate on Tanya.

The postcard received from her two days before had said, *Ignore the blue skies. The mistral has been blowing for all week and the kids are hyper.* Les parents *have pushed off to Italy with friends, and I'm stuck at the above address going quietly insane. Help.*

Trouble is I've no real help to give, Chloe thought, as she attached the stamps and waited to receive her change. In fact it had been a hell of a struggle to try to sound cheerful and positive in return, when there was so much that she could not or would not mention, such as tomorrow night's dinner party at the Hall. At which, of course, Darius might or might not be present.

It's been one long whirl here, she'd written at last. *I've been riding, dog-walking and generally getting back into the local swing. My uncle is retiring quite soon, and I've been helping redecorate the house before they sell it.* She'd paused, chewing the end of her pen, then added, *When my feet eventually touch the ground, Ian and I plan to sit down quietly and sort out a date for the wedding.*

But would they? They dated a couple of times a week, but their relationship was still worryingly static, without even the anticipated invitation to the cottage anywhere on the horizon. And if as Ian had indicated, they needed to restart their relationship, it was a pretty muted affair, plodding along rather than sweeping her off her feet as she'd secretly hoped, and so badly needed to happen.

She wished she could confide in Tanya, but found herself jibbing at expressing her concerns in black-and-white, as if by doing so she would somehow set them in stone. Make them seem more serious than they really were.

After all, she reminded herself, marriage was for life and Ian was merely being sensible for both of them. Making sure they were sure.

But one of these days, Chloe told herself, when he wasn't

on call, or attending a meeting, or playing squash, she would seize the initiative and drive over there, taking the ingredients of a steak and wine dinner for two in a carrier bag.

'I hear the Grange is going on the market soon.' Mrs Thursgood intruded on her thoughts once again. 'So you'll be moving on too, I dare say.'

'I have plenty of time to make my own plans,' Chloe returned coolly, putting her coins in her purse and heading for the door.

Safely outside, she drew a deep breath. An errand at the post office often resembled an encounter with a grinding machine, she thought broodingly, and how nice it would be when she could brandish her engagement ring in front of her inquisitor and say, 'I'm going nowhere.'

Not a noble ambition, she admitted silently, but Mrs Thursgood effortlessly brought out the worst in her.

She returned slowly to her car. She'd planned to drive up to the Hall, as she'd done each day following Darius's departure ten days earlier and two increasingly irascible messages from Arthur, in order to exercise Orion. But the postmistress's comments on the reasons for his trip had managed to get under her guard in some unexpected and infuriating way.

It shouldn't have happened, she thought bitterly. Not when she'd been telling herself over and over again that his continuing absence was a relief. A case of 'out of sight, out of mind'.

But being forced to consider what he might indeed be doing while out of sight had aroused a sharp pang deep inside her, of which her damaged lip was only an outer sign.

It's none of my concern what he does, she told herself forcefully. He's a law unto himself and always has been. And if anyone should feel injured by his behaviour, it's certainly not me.

In the past few days, while she was out with Flare or

shopping in East Ledwick, she'd caught several glimpses of Lindsay Watson walking slowly along, her head bent, shoulders slumped and clearly deep in thought. And to judge by her body language, her thoughts were not particularly happy ones.

Chloe could imagine why. According to the village grapevine, Sir Gregory's condition was improving every day, which meant that he would soon not need a full-time nurse and Lindsay would be looking for another job.

Which meant that if she'd been entertaining hopes of securing Darius as a husband, her time could be running out, a situation not improved by his continuing absence in London. And maybe she too had her suspicions about what drew him there.

Maybe I should feel sympathy for her, thought Chloe. But somehow I can't. And anyway, I have my own problems.

When she arrived at the stable yard, she was surprised to see Samson out of his box, saddled and bridled but tied up securely. He clearly resented the restriction, moving restively, his head jerking and eyes rolling. Every glowing inch of him a magnificent challenge, thought Chloe, her heart missing a beat.

'Am I riding him today?' She couldn't keep the eagerness out of her voice, and Arthur snorted.

'Not on your life, gal. Mr Darius warned me before he went away that you weren't to be allowed anywhere near the nasty devil.'

'Oh,' said Chloe. 'Did he really?'

'Yes, missy, and he meant it, so you can take that look off your face. And Samson's going tomorrow, off to stud in Ireland, which I won't be sorry for.' He nodded severely. 'Tim Hankin, the gamekeeper's eldest boy has been coming over each afternoon to exercise the blighter, but he'll be early today as he has to rejoin his regiment. Off to Afghanistan again, seemingly.'

Chloe frowned. 'Tim? I don't think I know him.'

'Good lad,' said Arthur. 'But wild when he was a youngster. Mr Darius, being a pal of his, had to drag him out of all kinds of trouble, some worse than others.'

Chloe lifted her chin. She said coolly, 'It sounds to me like six of one and half a dozen of the other.'

'Does it?' said Arthur grimly. 'Then maybe you don't know as much about Mr Darius as you think, my girl. Now I'll finish tacking up Orion for you.'

Chloe leaned against the wall, watching Samson as he fidgeted, ears pricked, clearly bored and becoming irritable. In the stable she could hear Arthur's chiding voice telling Orion to stand still.

Seriously fast, she thought with longing, and jumps like an angel. Darius said so himself in the restaurant that night. But off to Ireland, so I may never get another chance.

And how dare he tell Arthur to warn me off, as if I was some stupid little novice who can't be trusted with a difficult horse? I'll show him—I'll show both of them that I can really ride. But I won't go too far—just down to the first paddock and back in order to make my point.

She began to walk towards Samson, who acknowledged her approach by curling back his lip to show his teeth.

She said softly, 'Come on, beautiful. Show me how nice you can be.'

But *nice* did not seem to be a word that Samson understood. As she approached, he began to stamp, swishing his tail, his nostrils flaring ominously. Chloe halted, trying to quell her sudden apprehension.

Dangerous, she thought. Dangerous and unpredictable. Both attributes which had attracted her once before and almost led her to disaster.

She took a deep breath. If you get the better of Samson, she thought, then maybe you can also conquer this ludicrous obsession with Darius, and put it behind you where it belongs, once and for all.

It's something you have to prove to yourself, for heaven's sake, if you're to have any hope for the future.

As she got closer, Samson began to sidle around, trying to jerk loose from his tethering ring probably in order to lunge at her.

Murmuring nonsense in a low, soothing voice, wondering which of them she was trying to calm most, herself or the horse, Chloe warily adjusted the girth and the stirrups.

And then, as if by magic, all the angry restless movements were suddenly stilled and his head even drooped a little.

Well, what do you know? thought Chloe. Maybe all he ever needed was a woman's touch.

Very gingerly, she untied him and, without having lost a hand, swung herself up into the saddle.

For a moment, everything was quiet, but it was only the lull before the storm as Samson's powerful muscles bunched and, with a squeal of pure rage, he wheeled round then reared up, in an attempt to throw her off his back and into oblivion.

His hooves clattered down and he went into a series of fierce bucks, forcing her to cling on desperately, winding a hand in his mane in addition to the reins.

Every atom of concentration in her body was fixed on staying in the saddle, because she knew that if she was thrown, she would be kicked and trampled. That the least she could expect was serious injury.

She was half blind with fright, almost deafened by the noise of his drumming, relentless hooves, overwhelmed by her helplessness in the face of such fury, and yet, somewhere in her consciousness, there seemed to be men's voices shouting.

Someone was there, a stranger, tall and broad-shouldered, seizing the bridle as Arthur arrived on the other side, both of them clinging there, fighting Samson to a breathless, swearing halt, while another pair of strong arms reached up and dragged Chloe without gentleness out of the saddle, hauling her back across the yard and out of the range of those viciously kicking back legs.

Sobbing drily, wordlessly with relief, she looked up into Darius's white face. Saw the emerald blaze of his eyes, felt herself scorched by an anger that left Samson as a mere beginner, and knew that any thought of safety was an illusion.

He said between his teeth, 'Hell, woman, are you suicidal or just bloody insane?'

She tried to speak, to explain, but no sound would come from the tightness of her throat. His arms were iron, caging her, making her listen as his voice went on, soft and menacing, never repeating himself, as his words seemed to flay the skin from her bones.

At last she began to cry, the scalding tears pouring silently and remorselessly down her pale face, and his grasp slackened.

He said with great weariness, 'Oh, God,' and looked across to where Samson stood, defeated and sullen, between his two warders.

He said, 'Tim, Miss Benson's car's just outside. Drive her back to Axford Grange, will you, and I'll see you for a farewell drink at the Butchers Arms in an hour.'

She began to say that she could drive herself, trying to snatch back some atom of dignity from the situation, but the look he sent her stopped her in her tracks.

Tim Hankin's hand under her elbow was firm, but there was kindness in it too, and she went with him without further protest.

They were outside the Hall grounds and on the road to the village when he eventually spoke, his tone gentle.

'You don't want to take what Darius said too much to heart, Miss Benson. Yes, you did a silly thing, but his bark's always been worse than his bite, as I have cause to know.'

Chloe was blotting her face with a handful of tissues from the glove compartment. She said chokingly, 'No-one's ever spoken to me like that before. As if they—hated me.'

'Well,' he said. 'Fear takes people in different ways. And he was much rougher on me, I promise you, because I deserved it more.'

She said, sniffing, 'I can't believe that.'

'Then you'd be wrong.' He pulled the car onto the verge, and switched off the engine. 'It's not something I'm proud of, but maybe you need to hear it.'

He paused. 'It was a long time ago.' His voice was quiet and serious. 'We'd always been mates from young kids, Darius and me. But he'd been away—school then university—and I was bored, being expected to follow in Dad's footsteps as a gamekeeper and not sure it was what I wanted, so I got in with a bad crowd.

'Darius found out somehow—he always could—and discovered what they were up to. I'd not wanted to get involved because it was against the law and vile too, but I didn't know how to break free. I knew the kind of men they were and what they'd do to me if I tried.'

Chloe gasped. 'Was it—dog fighting?'

'Yes.' Tim Hankin spoke heavily. 'Darius knew that the police were tracking the gang organising it and there was going to be a raid. He also knew what it would do to Mum and Dad if I was caught with them, and he came to find me. Got me out some way, God knows how, and we headed for home, miles across country dodging the police who were everywhere. He was taking one hell of a risk for me.

'When we'd gone far enough to be safe, he went for me. Called me every name under the sun and a few more even I hadn't heard of. Then he hit me. Knocked me down, and I didn't even try to defend myself because I knew I'd asked for it and more.

'Then we sat down and talked, and the next day he drove me to the nearest recruiting office and I joined up, got into a regiment where I could work with horses.'

She said, 'There were—rumours—afterwards, about Darius. That he was the one going to dog fights.'

'I know that, and I'm sorry for it. But he never cared much about local gossip or what people thought of him.'

He gave her a sober look. 'However, I could have ended up in jail, Miss Benson, and you could be laid in that yard with your neck broken, and how could he ever have lived with that? Think about it.'

He restarted the car. 'And now I'll get you home.'

CHAPTER TEN

'PAPERWORK?' Chloe repeated. 'You have to catch up on paperwork? Oh, Ian, surely not.'

'Look.' His voice down the phone sounded harassed. 'I'll still be coming to the wretched dinner party. I just won't be able to pick you up first. But there's no real problem, surely, when you can go with your aunt and uncle?'

'No,' Chloe agreed with an effort. 'Of course not.'

But that's not the point, she longed to shout at him. I wanted to arrive with you, as one half of a couple, so I wouldn't have to face Darius tonight on my own. I was relying on you to be with me from the start.

And I can't even tell you why without admitting the lethally stupid thing I did trying to ride Samson. Maybe Darius was right and I did take leave of my senses. But I can't bear anyone else to know, especially Aunt Libby and Uncle Hal.

They hadn't been at home when she'd returned the day before. A scribbled note left on the kitchen table explained they'd gone into East Ledwick to talk to an estate agent, and her lunch—a pan of home-made vegetable soup keeping warm on the range, fresh bread and some good cheese—was waiting.

She only managed a few spoonfuls of soup, her churning stomach resisting any thought of solid food.

She was still shaking with reaction to the abominable risk

she'd taken and the consequent scene in the stable yard. Nor could she stop crying. It didn't matter how many times she tried to tell herself that Darius had no right to speak to her like that, she still knew in her heart that the fault was hers and she deserved every damning word.

Her immediate thought was to invent some illness in order to avoid the following night's dinner party, and only the conviction that Darius would know she was faking it kept her on track. The prospect of having to endure more of his icy scorn when they did eventually meet was more than she could bear.

Her battle with Samson had left her physically as well as mentally bruised, so when she had cleared lunch away, she went upstairs and indulged in a long, hot bath.

But if the warm water eased her body, it also freed her mind, and she found herself thinking back over everything Tim Hankin had said, especially with regard to the illegal dog-fighting ring and the role Darius had played in it, contrary to all reports.

She had to be glad that he hadn't been involved in anything so disgusting, but while he might have been misjudged over that, there was still plenty to set to his account, she told herself resolutely. He hadn't suddenly turned into the Archangel Gabriel. And there was certainly no need for her to make excuses for him.

She found some arnica tablets in the bathroom cabinet, and remembered too how Darius had once offered her the same remedy.

For a moment she stood, staring into space, the small bottle clutched in her hand. Then she took a deep breath and said aloud, 'I will not think about him. I will not.'

But it was obvious that she needed something to take her mind off the past few hours and hard work was usually the best diversion, she thought as she recalled Aunt Libby saying that the borders in the front garden needed weeding.

Accordingly, she put on old jeans and a tee shirt and went out to tackle them.

'Kerb appeal,' she muttered as she dealt with a persistent dandelion. 'And I hope the punters appreciate it.'

Her aunt and uncle were certainly appreciative of her efforts, especially as three valuations of the Grange had been scheduled for the start of the following week. But, over supper, they also began to enquire, albeit tactfully and gently, about her own plans, and she could tell them nothing.

It's time Ian and I stopped shilly-shallying, she told herself when she was in her room, having offered gardening fatigue as an excuse for an early night and an escape from further questions. If I'd had my wedding to plan, I'd have had no time to waste on exercising other people's horses, and saved myself a load of grief.

Against the odds, she slept soundly, and woke determined to be positive.

'I'm getting my hair done in honour of tonight's dinner party,' Aunt Libby announced over breakfast. 'Shall I ask Denise if she can fit you in too?'

Chloe shook her head. 'I'll give myself a shampoo, thanks, and just leave it loose.' She paused, smiling. 'The way Ian likes it.'

Her aunt gave her a swift glance then looked back at her plate. 'Just as you wish, my dear,' she said equably. 'I presume he'll be driving you to the Hall tonight.'

'Indeed he will,' said Chloe.

Only now he wouldn't, so there was embarrassment to add to the disappointment of his phone call, she realised as she busied herself preparing a ham salad for lunch.

Her uncle was later than usual and came in apologising. 'I've been up at the Hall,' he said. 'In case a shot of something was needed to get that damned horse of Andrew Maynard's into the box for transit. But Darius had summoned a couple of grooms over from that stud farm of his in Ireland, and they got the job done.'

'Oh.' Chloe set down his plate with more than usual care, aware her heartbeat had quickened nervously. 'I—heard Samson was going.' She tried to keep her tone casual, wondering if anything had been said about her visit the day before, and steeling herself for another dressing down, but Uncle Hal was serving himself from a dish of new potatoes with apparent unconcern, so she seemed to have been spared.

Yet that made the prospect of the evening ahead no more enticing, although she felt that she could be reasonably satisfied with her appearance at least. She was wearing a favourite dress in a close-fitting silky fabric that enhanced every slender curve, knee-length, long-sleeved and scoop-necked in a dramatic shade of deep red. Her lips and nails had been painted to match, and she had the antique garnet-and-pearl drops that had been part of her twenty-first birthday present, in her ears.

Fighting colours, she thought ironically, as she viewed herself in the mirror. Nothing even slightly penitential, although she had reluctantly decided that some word of regret for her escapade the previous day would be appropriate if a suitable opportunity occurred, at the same time, crossing her fingers that it wouldn't. And she knew that she should also be thankful that her stupidity hadn't been mentioned.

Only she didn't feel even remotely grateful. Just terribly apprehensive.

Although she told herself a dozen times that she was overreacting, it was a feeling that somehow, in spite of her best efforts, refused to go away.

Chloe had hoped that Ian would deal quickly with the VAT returns or whatever was holding him up, and be at the Hall, waiting for her.

But one glance round the drawing room soon disabused her of that notion, and her heart sank.

Oh, Ian where are you when I need you? she whispered under her breath.

Sir Gregory was seated in a high-backed armchair beside the fireplace. While he was undoubtedly resplendent in a dark green velvet smoking jacket, his face was sunken with one side of his mouth turned down a little. And he appeared, Chloe thought instantly, to have shrunk in some odd way.

Or perhaps he just seemed smaller in contrast to the tall young man in the charcoal suit and pale grey brocade waistcoat, standing beside him and resting a casual arm on the back of his father's chair.

And who was now walking forward, smiling. 'Mrs Jackson. It's a pleasure to see you again. And Mr Jackson.' They all shook hands, then Darius let his glance drift past them to the girl standing in silence behind them.

'Chloe,' he said, inclining his head with cool politeness.

She returned a breathless, 'Good evening,' joined her aunt and uncle in their polite greetings to Sir Gregory, then turned away rather too hastily to speak to Dr Vaughan, the head of the neighbourhood GP practice and his wife. The vicar was there too with Mrs Squires, and so were Hugo Burton and Prunella Burton, the local MP and his wife, and by the time she'd greeted them all, and taken a glass of orange juice from the tray of drinks being brought round by a maid, she was beginning to feel rather more comfortable. But she would only be able to relax properly, she told herself, when Ian arrived.

Which he seemed in no hurry to do, and she could only hope he'd put in an appearance before dinner was actually announced.

When the drawing room door eventually opened, she turned hopefully, but it was to see Lindsay Watson walk into the room. She was wearing a dark navy dress with a white starched collar and cuffs. There was a small silver watch pinned to her breast pocket, and her blond hair was drawn back into a severe bun.

On the surface, she was every inch the calm, efficient nurse, but her eyes were very bright and her face unusually flushed.

But why wouldn't she be looking a little flustered? Chloe thought, taking a gulp of orange juice to ease the sudden dryness in her throat, if she's aiming to be the next Lady Maynard and everyone in the room knows it?

Lindsay went straight to Sir Gregory, bending over him solicitously, and he nodded, smiling with an obvious effort.

Uncle Hal came over to Chloe. 'Just what is Ian playing at?' he asked in a displeased undertone. 'I've tried to phone him, but I can't get a signal in here.'

'I'll go out on the terrace and text him,' Chloe said quickly. 'Perhaps he's been called out to an emergency.'

'Then why didn't he ring and say so?' Uncle Hal demanded with inexorable logic, and Chloe could not think of an answer.

She slipped out through the French windows and went over to the balustrade, but she'd barely begun her message when she heard the crunch of footsteps on gravel and saw Ian appear round the corner of the house on the path below her, his face moody and preoccupied.

She leaned over the balustrade. 'Ian—where on earth have you been? And what are you doing, anyway, coming in this way?'

He glanced up with a start. 'Oh—Chloe.' He gave an uneven laugh. 'I forgot this was a social occasion and parked round by the stables. Force of habit, I guess.'

She drew a deep breath. 'Well, at least you're here. I was beginning to worry.'

He shrugged almost defensively. 'I was busy. I just—lost track of time.'

'Yes,' she said. 'Yes, I understand.'

Except that I don't. I don't understand any of this, and I'm even more scared now than I was earlier, and I need you to take me in your arms and tell me that everything's going to be all right. I need to walk back into that room with my hand in yours and make a joke about you getting lost.

But I already know in my heart that's not going to happen. That somehow I'm on my own here.

And she thought of Darius's cold green glance reaching her across the room, and suppressed a shiver.

She lifted her chin. 'So,' she said. 'Let's go in and have dinner.'

As Aunt Libby had prophesied, the food was a dream, and even Chloe's persistent feeling of unease could put up no real resistance to its allure.

Ian was seated beside Lindsay Watson on the opposite side of the table and while they seemed to have little to say to each other, Chloe noticed with relief that he was chatting readily enough to Mrs Burton, his other neighbour. But he was also, she saw, enjoying more of the excellent wine being served than was wise.

Darius too appeared fully occupied at the far end of the table, entertaining Aunt Libby on one side and Mrs Vaughan on the other.

At the same time, Chloe was assailed at intervals during the long meal by a sharp tingle of awareness, warning her almost starkly that he was looking at her. In return, she tried hard to seem oblivious and did not allow herself as much as a glance in his direction.

Yet, all too often, she found herself remembering the brief snatch of conversation between Darius and Lindsay that she'd inadvertently overheard on the way into dinner.

'Why the uniform, Lindsay?' he'd asked. 'You're supposed to be off duty tonight, remember?'

'Because I thought it was more appropriate.' She did not look at him or smile. 'Under the circumstances.'

Clearly, he'd expected her to present herself as his future wife rather than his father's paid carer, thought Chloe, biting her lip.

When the meal was over, Sir Gregory rose slowly and with obvious difficulty and apologised for not joining the party in the drawing room for coffee.

'Dr Vaughan will tell you that I must ration my excitements for the foreseeable future,' he told them.

Chloe went upstairs with the rest of the women to comb her hair and renew her lipstick, but on her way down again she saw Darius standing at the foot of the stairs, and realised he was waiting for her.

She halted, disconcerted, before reluctantly continuing her descent, and his sardonic smile told her that her hesitation was not lost on him.

'My father is resting in his library,' he said. 'However, he would like to talk to you, if you can spare him a few minutes.'

'He wants to see me?' She could not hide her surprise.

'I've just said so.'

She stood for a moment, fiddling with the clasp of her evening bag. 'Is he also going to tell me off about Samson?'

'Good God, no.' His tone was short. 'You think I mentioned that to him? What the hell do you take me for?'

'I don't think I know any more.' She took a deep breath. 'But, while I have the chance, I need to say that I'm sorry for trying to ride him. I knew perfectly well that I shouldn't.'

'Yes,' Darius said. 'But I gather you're not wholly to blame. Because for you to hear that I'd said exactly that was like showing a red rag to a bull, according to Arthur, who's been kicking himself ever since for telling you.'

'So now I'm a bull.' She pretended to wince. 'But thank you too for not mentioning it to my uncle—or anyone else.'

He said quietly, 'The matter was dealt with in house. And I've never been a squealer, Chloe.'

'No.' She paused, then said in a rush, 'Tim told me what you did for him—about the dog-fighting.'

'Did he?' He shrugged. 'Well, it hardly matters. It was a very long time ago.'

'Yes,' she said. 'But people thought that you were involved in it, not Tim.'

'Yes,' he said. 'They did. But I managed to live with it.' He gave a faint smile. 'Or maybe I should say away from it.'

'What do you mean?'

He said flatly, 'That it helped convince me that Willowford was not for me, and my place was elsewhere.'

She said uncertainly, 'Yet you're back now.'

'For the time being.' His voice was curt again. 'And we're keeping my father waiting.'

In spite of the warmth of the evening, Sir Gregory was sitting with a rug over his knees beside a small fire. His eyes were closed, but one hand was beating a restless tattoo on the arm of his chair.

Darius said gently, 'Here's Chloe, Father.'

'Good,' Sir Gregory said after a pause. 'That's good. Please sit down, my dear.'

As Chloe took the seat opposite, she heard the library door shut and realised Darius had left them alone together.

There was a silence, then Sir Gregory said, 'My wife used to say you would be a beauty, my child, and she was quite right.'

Chloe flushed. 'She was always very kind to me.'

He said haltingly, 'She had great hopes for you. Believed you should be allowed to stretch your wings and fly.' He paused. 'She talked to you, I think, about her early life. The cities and foreign embassies that became her home?'

Chloe smiled. 'Yes,' she said gently. 'She did. She made it all sound wonderful—exotic, exciting.'

'She loved to travel. Perhaps even she did not realise how much it meant to her.' He lifted a handkerchief to the corners of his mouth. Went on slowly, 'When we first met and married, we planned to continue in the same way. To see the rest of the world together. Then my father died very suddenly, and we were obliged to come back here instead.

'And, of course, everything changed. A house like this—an estate—brings its responsibilities with it. We could not just leave it behind and go. Or so I believed. But then I was born and brought up here, and although I knew it was a backwater, it was *my* backwater, and I loved it.'

He sighed. 'Then the boys were born, and that seemed another reason to build our lives around the home we were making here.

'I thought Margaret shared my contentment, but in reality, she felt stifled by village life and its obligations. Being constantly under a spotlight. Eventually, Willowford began to seem like a prison to her.'

Chloe stirred uneasily. 'Sir Gregory, I don't think…'

He held up a hand. 'Please, my dear, I need to tell you these things. My wife would have wished me to. Because you made the break when you went to university and afterwards, just as she'd always hoped you would. You took flight away from this small world.

'Yet now, my son tells me, you have come back to be married and to settle here, so it is vital for you to be sure that this is really the life for you.

'That it's the only possible future you can see for yourself.'

He paused. 'I believe you once wanted to be a writer. Has that been forgotten about?'

She stared at him, her breathing quickening, sharply, inexplicably. 'No, not entirely,' she said jerkily. 'But I can always write after I'm married. I'll have more time then. And Willowford is the only real home I've ever had. I—I always meant to return.'

He leaned forward with an effort, his gaze boring into hers. 'And is it just as you remember, or has it changed? Are you even the same person that went away?'

'Yes,' she said huskily. 'I am. And I admit that things here are different in many ways. But that doesn't matter because I've come back to find the man I love, and be happy with him, just as I've always dreamed.'

There was a silence, then he said, 'Ah,' and leaned back against the cushions piled behind him. He turned his head slowly and gazed at the flames burning in the fireplace. 'Then may your dreams come true, my dear. And now I wish you goodnight.'

Chloe stood outside the library door, her arms wrapped defensively across her body, as she tried to make sense of what had just happened. She would have sworn that Sir Gregory was barely aware of her existence, and yet he'd talked as if he knew and was concerned about her.

As, apparently, Lady Maynard had once been. A woman whose own wings had been clipped by duty, but who had always longed for the larger world she'd left behind. Who'd found village life stifling and oppressive.

But I'm not like that, Chloe whispered to herself. I don't want to escape. Because I do belong here. I do!

'Chloe.' The thick carpet had muffled the sound of his approach, and she gasped, taking an instinctive step backwards.

'I know my way back to the drawing room.' She faced him, her heart pounding unevenly. 'You really didn't have to collect me.'

'I came to bring you a message,' Darius returned equably.

'Your boyfriend seemed a little the worse for wear after his double brandy, so your aunt and uncle decided to take him home. He can collect his car tomorrow.'

'They've already left?' Chloe shook her head, mortification over Ian's behaviour warring with other concerns. 'Then how am I supposed to get back to the Grange? Or am I allowed three guesses?' she added bitterly.

'I think you'd lose.' He sounded faintly amused. 'The Vaughans live in your direction. They say they'll be happy to drop you off.'

It was the last thing she'd expected to hear, and she managed a weak, 'Oh. Well—thank you,' in return.

It was time she returned to the drawing room and other people, but Darius was still there, not exactly blocking the way, but certainly too close for comfort.

She took a deep breath. 'Ian doesn't usually drink too much,' she declared. 'He—he's been under a lot of stress lately.'

'I can imagine,' Darius said silkily. 'Brought on by the prospect of his approaching nuptials no doubt.'

I led with my chin there, Chloe thought biting her lip savagely. Will I never learn?

'Who knows?' she said. 'You may be tempted to hit the bottle yourself when your own day comes.'

'Unlikely,' he said. 'I've no wish to bring a hangover to my wedding night.' He smiled at her, his gaze unhurriedly brushing aside the cling of her dress as if it didn't exist. 'On the contrary,' he went on musingly. 'My wife will receive my sober and undivided attention.'

'And that,' Chloe said stonily, 'is altogether too much information.' She stepped forward. 'Would you excuse me, please? I need to find the Vaughans. I can't miss out on another lift.'

'Of course not,' he said. 'But what are you going to do, Chloe, when you have no more places left to run to or people to rescue you? What will happen when you realise you've made the biggest mistake of your life?'

'I already did that,' she said with sudden hoarseness. 'Seven years ago when I was fool enough to listen to the things you said to me—to let you anywhere near me.'

'Rather an exaggeration, my sweet.' His tone was light, but his face seemed carved from stone in the dim light of the passage. 'Any damage caused was far from irreparable. And I was the bigger fool to let you off so lightly. It won't happen next time.'

'Next time?' Her attempt at a laugh sounded as if she was choking. 'Have you taken leave of your senses?'

'Not yet,' Darius said very quietly. 'But when I do, I'll take you with me.' His hand snaked out and caught her arm, pulling her towards him. His fingers slid under the shoulder of her dress, baring the pale skin beneath it for the burn of his mouth.

The stark male heat of him pressed against her was igniting her quivering body, racing through her bloodstream and melting her bones.

His lips moved downwards, pushing aside the fragile lace that cupped her breast, in order to quest its hardening nipple and suckle it with heart-stopping sensuality.

'No. Oh, God, no.' The words seemed to come from nowhere, torn from her aching throat. Her hands thrust at him in an attempt to distance herself before her self-betrayal became complete.

His fingers wound themselves in her hair, pulling back her head so that he could look down into her white, desperate face and tormented eyes.

He said harshly, 'Stay with me. Stay tonight. I'll make some excuse to the Vaughans.'

'No.' Chloe dragged her dress into place with shaking

hands. 'Never. And you have no right to ask. Because I hate you. You—you disgust me.'

'In other circumstances,' Darius said very softly, 'I would take you to bed right now and make you retract every word you've just uttered. As it is, my little hypocrite, I have to get back to my guests. However, I hope you have had a pleasant evening, and that you derive equal enjoyment from the sleepless night alone that's waiting for you.'

He bent his head and let his mouth brush hers gently but with an agonising slowness that was somehow worse than any kind of force.

He said, 'Until we meet again, Chloe.'

And left her.

CHAPTER ELEVEN

'I wasn't drunk,' Ian said irritably. 'But I admit I was probably over the limit. Although that was hardly my fault,' he added defensively. 'Perhaps our gracious host shouldn't have topped up my glass quite so often.'

Or maybe you should have simply put your hand over your glass to stop him, like all the other drivers, thought Chloe, but kept silent.

She said quietly, 'I'm not having a go—truly. I think I'm just disappointed that we didn't get to spend more time together.' She paused. 'I seem to see so little of you these days.'

'Well, with your uncle's retirement looming up, I guess that's inevitable.' Ian shrugged. 'I have a lot to learn in the way of office management, for one thing.'

And what are the other things? Chloe asked herself. It seemed wiser, however, not to pursue the topic, while Darius's mocking words about the possible cause of Ian's stress still twisted painfully in her mind.

But she would rather think about them than their incredible, shameful aftermath in his arms. And the implied threat in his parting remark which still made her shiver.

Once alone, she'd gone straight to the downstairs cloakroom, and splashed cold water on her wrists in an attempt to calm her tumultuous pulses, but there was little she could do about her flushed face and fevered eyes.

When she got back to the drawing room the party was breaking up, and her faint dishevelment seemed fortunately to go unnoticed in the flurry of goodbyes.

She'd expected to face some strong words about Ian's conduct from Uncle Hal when she got back to the Grange but, to her surprise, neither he nor Aunt Libby mentioned it, preferring apparently to discuss the delicious food and Sir Gregory's undoubted improvement in health.

She'd also anticipated that Ian would be eating his share of humble pie when she saw him next, but she was wrong about that too, she thought, sighing.

Pressure of work had reduced the already limited amount of time they spent together. They'd met for drinks a couple of times, had dinner in East Ledwick once, and been to the cinema to see a film during which Ian had gone to sleep.

All in all, it did not seem an appropriate time to raise the subject of their postponed engagement, although the situation could not be allowed to drag on indefinitely.

After all, she had come back to Willowford for him, she told herself, and now, more than ever, she needed the safeguard of his ring on her hand and the public declaration of commitment that would justify her return.

It should also be sufficient to keep Darius at bay both physically and mentally, she thought fiercely, recalling the shaming fantasies that had made her toss and turn all night long, just as he'd predicted.

Also, in less than ten days' time there would be the ordeal of the Birthday Ball to be endured with all its particular resonances that she would still give so much to forget.

I can't look back, she thought. I dare not. And I must never let him near me again.

I have to plan for the future and disregard everything else, including all the strange things Sir Gregory said to me the other night. Particularly those.

And wondered why they suddenly seemed so important.

'So that young nurse is leaving the Hall, I hear,' said Mrs Thursgood. 'Must mean that the old gentleman is properly on the mend.' She gave Chloe a bland smile. 'You won't be so sorry to see her go, I dare say.'

'I'm certainly glad Sir Gregory is well enough not to need anyone,' Chloe returned carefully, aware that her heart had skipped a beat at the news.

'And that's not all,' the other woman went on. 'That other one—Mr Andrew's widow—is coming back.' She nodded in satisfaction at Chloe's startled expression. 'She'll be here the day after tomorrow for the Ball, by all accounts. So, there's a turn up for the books, and no mistake. I never thought we'd set eyes on her again.'

She sniffed. 'But it's all forgive and forget, seemingly. And maybe we'll be having another wedding, if Mr Darius decides to do the right thing by her, that is.'

'Yes,' Chloe said, in a voice she didn't recognise. 'Perhaps so.'

She paid for what she'd bought as if she was on autopilot, and went out into the relentless sunshine, releasing the leash of a delighted Flare from the rail provided for the purpose.

Penny, she thought in stupefaction. Penny, no longer in disgrace, and returning to Willowford to be with her lover— the man for whom she'd once abandoned everything. To be reinstated—accepted as Sir Gregory's daughter-in-law all over again. It couldn't possibly be true—could it?

But if it was, if the incredible, the unthinkable, was really happening, then small wonder that Lindsay Watson had decided to cut her losses and go.

Yet, I can't, she thought numbly, staring down at the footpath with eyes that saw nothing, as she began to walk out of the village, heading for the fields the dog loved.

Because I have to stay here somehow and watch it take place. Live with the knowledge that she and Darius are together and happy. As they may have been all this time.

Oh, dear God, to be confronted by it all on a daily basis and have to pretend that it doesn't matter, because I have my own life. To make everyone believe that I don't care. To try to make myself believe it.

What am I going to do? How can I possibly bear it?

She stopped dead in the middle of the lane, shocked by what she was thinking. Horrified by the sheer enormity of the revelation that had come to her at last, and was now tearing her apart.

The realisation that the man she'd really fallen in love with seven years ago—the man she had never ceased to want in her secret heart, despite everything he'd done—was Darius Maynard.

That it had always been him and always would be.

That all her efforts to rip her memories of him, her longing for him out of her mind had been totally in vain. That they were what drew her like a magnet back to Willowford, in spite of the time and distance between them, because one day she'd known she would find him here.

I must be insane, she thought with a kind of desperation. Because this isn't happening to me. It can't be. I won't allow it. I came back to Ian, to make a home with him. That was the plan for my life—wasn't it?

Feeling safe, knowing that he was waiting for me. That I could trust him to make everything all right.

Telling myself over and over again that I loved him. That I cared for him in a way that was good—and real, knowing he was kind and reliable, and that I would never have to worry about being hurt again.

She took a deep, wrenching breath, recognising that she'd treated all these hopes as certainties, wrapping them round her like some kind of security blanket, and hiding there. Unable—unwilling—to face the truth about her inmost feelings.

But just how secret had they really been? she wondered, as she went over her interview with Sir Gregory once again. Was he aware of her brief, wretched involvement with Darius seven years ago, and had he been trying to warn her that she still had nothing to hope for and that she would have done better to stay away for good?

Judging by her undisguised disapproval of Darius, Aunt Libby too must have guessed, and done her best to deflect her vulnerable niece from inevitable heartbreak.

And had Penny also known, and maybe even encouraged Darius to pay attention to a moonstruck teenager in order to conceal what was really going on between herself and her brother-in-law?

Although, she certainly wouldn't have expected matters to escalate towards a full-scale seduction, unless, of course, sexual fidelity didn't weigh very heavily with either of them.

Perhaps to Darius, I'm simply unfinished business, Chloe thought, feeling sick. A way to amuse himself while waiting to be reunited with Penny.

But at least the whole pitiful situation seemed to have escaped Mrs Thursgood's far-reaching antennae, although that was little enough to be thankful for.

Flare barked sharply, pulling at her leash, eager to resume her walk, startling Chloe out of her unhappy reverie and back to the immediate present.

Oh, God, she thought guiltily, realising she was still standing like a statue in the middle of the lane, if a car had come round the corner at speed, it couldn't have avoided us, and Flare at least doesn't deserve it.

She moved hurriedly over to the verge and set off again, her mind teeming endlessly, wretchedly.

'What am I going to do?' she whispered under her breath. 'What *can* I do?'

She remembered she'd once thought of trying to persuade Ian to move away and start again elsewhere. Now there seemed even less chance of his agreement, and maybe, now she'd faced up to her real feelings, she should cut Ian out of the equation altogether.

I've led him up the garden path for quite long enough, she thought, steeling herself, even if I meant it all for the very best, and would have done all I could to make him happy.

But if I'd loved him as I should, I would never have kept him waiting all this time. I'd have wanted to give myself—be his in every way, married or not. How could I not see that?

I've got everything so very wrong, she told herself. Treated him so badly. But now I must start putting it all right—for my own sake as well as his.

Because my next priority will be to contact my agency in London for a long-term job abroad in Europe or even America. Cut myself off completely and pray that time and distance will do its work.

Whatever happens here, she thought bleakly, I can't be around to witness it. And the fact that my aunt and uncle are moving away too will help, because their news will be about another place and other people.

She recalled how Sir Gregory had asked her if she was the same person who had gone away all those years ago.

I said I was and I am, she thought bitterly, swallowing past the harsh tightness in her throat. Which is my own private tragedy. Because I was cut to ribbons through loving Darius when I first left—when I went away to university. It took me a year just to get my head together and start to do some work. I was amazed they didn't throw me out.

He said the other night that he'd let me off lightly, but it isn't true, because he nearly destroyed me.

Now, here I am, loving him still, and facing heartbreak all over again. And I haven't even the excuse of being a teenager any more.

Flare was tugging her towards a favourite gateway, and she lifted the iron latch, unclipped the leash and let the dog bound into the empty meadow beyond, while she followed more slowly. The grass sloped down to a narrow stream and Chloe sank down in the shade of the solitary copper beech which grew on its edge, leaning thankfully back against its trunk.

Flare splashed straight into the water, emerging damp, joyous and, after she'd shaken herself vigorously, ready for a game with the squeaky toy which she knew her silent companion had in the pocket of her jeans.

She's so much wiser than me, thought Chloe, caught between tears and laughter. She knows that life simply goes on.

And however I may feel now, one day there'll be another place far from here with a tree at my back and sunlight on water, and I'll be healed. Or that's what I have to believe. And then I may even be ready for a love and trust that will last for the rest of my life.

Her dress, classically strapless and full-skirted in jade-green taffeta, was hanging on the outside of the wardrobe. It was the last thing she'd seen before going to sleep the night before, and the first she glimpsed when she woke on the morning of the ball itself.

She sat up, hugging her knees, and warily contemplating its glowing magnificence through the shrouding plastic cover.

No Lizzie Bennet lookalike this time, and not what she'd intended to buy at all.

It had been extremely expensive for one thing, and wearing it would almost certainly be a one-off. A dramatic statement that could not be repeated.

But there would never be any need for that, she thought, because in twenty four hours it would all be over. And the new Chloe Benson would be preparing once more for flight to a new life, having first sloughed off the half-truths and pathetic self deceptions of the old one. So maybe it was worth it.

Of course, there were still hurdles to be negotiated, like the essential long talk with her aunt and uncle, even if she could not be entirely frank with them about her motives for leaving.

A change of heart, she told herself. That was what she would say. And it was at least an approximation of the truth.

But Ian would have to be told first, and in spite of the personal difficulties they'd experienced since her return, she was not going to find it easy. Because she'd seen him for a drink the previous evening, and it had been strangely like old times in so many ways, with Ian quietly relaxed and in a reminiscent mood, as well as holding her with real tenderness as they said goodnight.

It had made her see why she'd thought she could make it work, she admitted ruefully. Even if the need for him—the ache for his touch—had never actually come between her and sleep. Which, in itself, should have warned her.

It was only when he'd driven off that she realised they hadn't actually finalised what time he would pick her up for the ball.

Their last date, she thought, even though she had no real right to be going anywhere as his partner. Not any more. But she needed to dance, laugh and look like a girl without a care in the world. Someone with nothing but a lifetime of happiness in front of her.

The alternative, of course, was to invent some minor ailment—a stomach upset perhaps—and cry off. But she had not given that serious consideration.

Because she needed to know, she told herself. To see Darius and Penny together, the future baronet and his lady, and understand once and for all that she had nothing to hope for and it was time to draw a line and move on. After she had said a silent and final farewell.

She felt her throat muscles contract harshly, and closed her eyes, deliberately putting Darius out of her mind. She would deal with that situation when she had to, and not before.

She would think instead of other—minor—leave-takings. People and places she would miss. And, of course, saying goodbye to Flare.

Lizbeth Crane's wrist was better now, and her husband had returned from Brussels the previous day, so her dog-walking services were no longer required.

'You've been an absolute star.' Mrs Crane had hugged her exuberantly. 'I don't know what I'd have done without you.'

'I was happy to do it,' Chloe assured her. She paused. 'I suppose I'll see you at the ball.'

'We wouldn't miss it,' said Lizbeth and hesitated in turn. 'Although there are all kinds of strange rumours concerning it floating round the village.' She gave Chloe an odd look. 'And some of them, if they were true, could cause the most terrible damage. But I'm sure it's all a pack of lies, and there's nothing to worry about.'

She shook her head. 'John's always said that, in more enlightened times, Mrs Thursgood would have been ducked in the village pond.'

'Almost certainly,' Chloe said, forcing a smile, and wondering just how far the gossip about Darius and herself had spread in the past few days, and what had triggered it.

But at least it did not seem to have reached Ian, she reflected now as she made herself get out of bed and off to the bathroom for her shower. And she could only hope it never would. She did not want to add to the hurt she was bound to inflict anyway.

But, in that case, why was she maintaining the illusion they were still a couple? How unkind and unfair was that? She had stifled her pangs of conscience by telling herself it was dire necessity for her to go to the ball with an escort.

Now she had to face facts. I'm using him, she thought unhappily, as the hot water streamed over her. And that's entirely wrong. I should have the guts to tell him first that it's over between us, but that, although it's a lot to ask, I'd still value his company this evening, and let him make the choice.

The chances were, of course, that he'd refuse, and angrily too. But that was a risk she'd have to take, even if it meant reverting to Plan B and staying away from the ball altogether.

'Is Ian on duty at the centre this morning?' she asked her uncle, who was swallowing the last of his coffee en route to the door.

'No, he asked if he could have the time off for some reason, so I'm covering for him.'

'Probably wants a rest before tonight's frivolity,' Chloe said lightly. It would be much easier, she thought, to talk at the cottage, although, ironically, it would be her first as well as her last visit to the Mark II version of it. But at least the alterations there were all Ian's doing, and she had no vested interest in it.

Uncle Hal snorted. 'Just as long as he's not indulging in some Dutch courage as well, as he obviously did before that dinner party,' he said drily, and left.

And just as long as nothing about tonight resembles that

dinner party in any way, shape or form, Chloe thought, sliding bread into the toaster.

She was just finishing breakfast when Aunt Libby bustled in looking, harassed. 'The agents have just rung to say they want to bring some people round at eleven o'clock for a viewing. And everywhere's such a mess.'

The house was fine, Chloe knew, as it had been for the previous three viewings, but her aunt needed it to be immaculate.

She rose, putting her crockery in the dishwasher. 'Then let's get cracking,' she said briskly. 'Give the place the hardsell treatment.'

'But you have an appointment at the Charm School in East Ledwick.'

'Yes, but not till half-past eleven. I can lend a hand here first.'

Although it meant she wouldn't have time to call on Ian on the way to the beauty salon as she'd planned, she thought. But the return trip would serve just as well. And maybe being manicured, pedicured and facialled first would provide her with a form of emotional body armour.

It was good to relax under the skilled hands of Bethany, the Charm School's owner, and by the time the face mask was being removed Chloe felt totally refreshed, and had rehearsed exactly what she needed to say to Ian.

Except that he wasn't there. The door of the cottage was locked, the curtains were half-drawn, and his car was gone.

I should have phoned first, Chloe told herself, as she went back to her own vehicle. Made sure he was around. Now I'll just have to catch him later.

The first thing she noticed when she arrived back at the Grange was a 'sold' sticker across the house agent's board in the garden.

'Wonderful news,' she called out as she entered the house. 'Is the champagne on ice?'

To her surprise, there was no reply. And when she walked into the kitchen, she found Aunt Libby sitting, staring into space, an untouched cup of coffee going cold on the table in front of her.

Oh, heavens, thought Chloe. It's suddenly hit her that it's done now, and there's no going back. And that leaving is going to be a bigger wrench than she bargained for.

She said gently, 'Listen, darling, it's all for the best, and I'm sure, in your heart, you know that. And you'll find another house you really love...'

But Mrs Jackson was shaking her head. 'It's got nothing to do with the house, Chloe. It's something—completely different.' She took a deep breath. 'Ian's been here. He arrived just after the other people had left.'

'Which explains why I missed him at the cottage.' Chloe refilled the kettle. 'I suppose he came to say what time he'd pick me up tonight.'

'No,' said her aunt. 'No, he didn't. Because he won't be going to the ball. He's off on a week's unpaid leave instead.' She was silent for a moment, then said in a sudden burst, 'Oh, Chloe, my dearest, he's gone away with Lindsay Watson—to be married.'

Chloe put the kettle down very carefully, her head whirling.

She said carefully, 'Ian—and Lindsay? I don't understand.'

'Oh, the gossip about them started not long after she arrived,' Mrs Jackson said bitterly. 'But I took no notice. They were both single, so I thought it was just—Willowford putting two and two together to make half a dozen.'

She paused. 'But the rumours seemed to persist. Only then you announced you were coming back, and you seemed so confident about your relationship that I decided to say nothing. That maybe you'd both had flings while you were apart, because that's how things are these days.'

'No,' Chloe said. 'I didn't.' *But not for Ian's sake, although I made myself believe that it was, but because I wanted someone else to the exclusion of all others.*

'I suspected that things weren't right between you,' Mrs Jackson went on. 'And wondered if I should say something, but I didn't want to interfere, not again, and now I wish that I had, although I had no real evidence. They were both very discreet.'

She reached across and extracted an envelope from beneath a pile of house agents' details.

'He brought you this letter,' she said, and put it on the table between them. She rose. 'I expect you'd rather read it alone.'

'Not at all.' Chloe shook her head. 'After all, I know what's in it.'

And I should have realised for myself from the start. All that business about getting to know each other all over again. The alterations to the cottage. Lindsay's hostility and the fact that Flare obviously knew her from somewhere. How could I not see it?

She remembered too Mrs Thursgood's warning about men going off the boil, and her comment on Lindsay's departure: 'You won't be sorry to see her go, I dare say.'

Everyone knew but me, she thought. *And I was too busy thinking about myself to notice.*

The envelope contained a single sheet of notepaper. 'Dear Chloe,' it ran. 'I know what you must think of me, and I can't possibly feel more of a louse than I already do. I should have told you from the outset that I'd met someone else, but it never seemed the right moment. My only excuse is that you were gone so long, and I was lonely.

'Trying not to upset you, I ended up hurting Lindsay instead, and matters came to a head just before the dinner party.

We had a terrible row and she told me to make up my mind once and for all or she was clearing out.

'She also said I shouldn't worry about you too much, because she'd bet good money that you had other fish to fry. Maybe you know what she means.

'Whatever, I wish you every happiness in the future. Ian.'

And good evening, friends, thought Chloe.

She passed the letter to Aunt Libby. 'There's nothing private. It's really just a confirmation of what he told you.'

'Oh, Chloe,' her aunt said when she'd read it. 'My dear, dear girl. I'm so very sorry.'

'Then you mustn't be.' Chloe retrieved the kettle and put it on the range. 'It's all for the best.' She paused. 'I suppose I had this image of Willowford in my mind as a haven, where everything would always be just the same, and I could step back into it whenever I wanted and find my place waiting for me.' She sighed. 'A kind of Garden of Eden in miniature.'

'With Mrs Thursgood as the snake,' Aunt Libby said grimly.

'How true,' Chloe agreed. 'But, of course, it was never like that. It was just wishful thinking on my part. And I was having my doubts about settling here permanently,' she added, choosing her words carefully. 'So maybe Ian's done me a favour.'

'I wish I could think so,' Aunt Libby said unhappily. 'You always seemed so certain that he was the one, and in many ways I was glad of it. Because I could feel justified about having intervened before, and tell myself I'd done the right thing.'

Chloe paused in spooning the coffee into the beakers. She said, 'I'm afraid you've lost me. When did you intervene, and why?'

Her aunt began to tidy the pile of papers, aligning them with acute precision. She said, 'He wrote, you see, wanting to contact you in London. And because I didn't answer his letter, he came back. He came here.'

Chloe was very still. She said huskily, 'Aunt Libby—are you—can you be talking about—Darius?'

Her aunt nodded jerkily. 'He said that he was going abroad almost immediately, but that he had to see you—to talk to you first. That there were things you had to know, that he needed to explain. He wanted your address, or just the name of your college. He—he almost begged.'

Chloe's throat was dry. 'And you said?'

'That he'd ruined enough lives already, and I wouldn't allow him to spoil yours,' Mrs Jackson said quietly. 'That I couldn't believe he had the gall to show his face in Willowford after what he'd done, and that he should go away and never return, because neither you nor anyone wanted to see him again.

'And I must have convinced him,' she added. 'Because he went.'

She paused. 'I don't know why I'm telling you—and at a time like this. I never intended to. And I suppose that's why I tried to be glad about Ian. Because I believed you'd be safe with him.'

'I did too,' said Chloe, and brought the coffee to the table. 'So we were both mistaken.' She bent and dropped a kiss on her aunt's greying hair. 'But you mustn't beat yourself up about Darius. You were absolutely right to send him away.' She took a deep breath. 'I—I shall always be grateful for that.'

And realised, her heart sinking, that it was only the first lie of many she would have to tell in the days to come in order to survive.

CHAPTER TWELVE

THE house seemed blessedly quiet as Chloe came downstairs.

In a way, Ian's departure, although something of a shock, had provided her with a perfect, indisputable excuse to miss the Birthday Ball, on the genuine grounds that she did not feel up to meeting people, and that she had a lot of thinking to do.

Except there was only one person she really wished to avoid. Two, she supposed wretchedly, if she counted Penny. As she knew she must.

Her need to think, of course, was nothing but the truth. She had plans to make, for one thing. And tomorrow the village's reaction to the news about Ian would break over her like a tidal wave. She therefore needed a story that would somehow show him in a reasonable light, while not presenting herself as a victim.

And she would be expected to comment on Penny's return too.

Lucky Mrs Thursgood, she thought. Two bombshells for the price of one.

However, it had taken serious perseverance to convince her aunt and uncle that she would be perfectly all right spending the evening alone. That she was planning to have a warm bath and an early night, and that they should go to the dance as arranged.

And even then they had fussed, asking worriedly if she was quite sure.

Uncle Hal, of course, had been incandescent about what he saw as Ian's betrayal, declaring he'd never been so deceived in anyone, and how glad he was that the partnership would soon be ending.

He had also received a note from Ian, left at the centre, announcing that he was taking a week's unpaid leave so that he and Lindsay could be married by special licence.

'I'd like to tell him to go on permanent leave,' he said grimly.

They were both so concerned for her, so convinced she was heroically concealing her grief over Ian's loss, and it was best they went on believing that. If she tried to tell them, or anyone else, that she'd been planning to end it anyway, her aunt and uncle would think she was trying desperately to salvage her pride. Other people would probably mutter, 'Sour grapes.'

And all of them would be wrong.

She poured herself a glass of wine and curled herself into a corner of the sofa, tucking the folds of her towelling dressing gown around her.

Yes, she was shaken by the day's events—not least by the voice in her head screaming endlessly, *Why—why—why?*

But the question, with its jagged, persistent pain which made her want to moan aloud, had nothing to do with Ian, but had been triggered by Aunt Libby's reluctant revelation that Darius had not simply walked away from her without a backward glance all those years ago.

On the contrary, that he'd even risked coming back to Willowfold, with all the possible repercussions his visit might lead to, in order to try and find her.

To explain...

But how? Chloe wondered wearily. How could one ever

explain the indefensible—the unforgivable? Or justify the destruction of his own brother's marriage and the misery that had been caused?

The ball tonight might be an attempt to paper over the gaping cracks in the Maynard dynasty, but how could it possibly succeed?

Lives had indeed been ruined, as Aunt Libby had said, but Chloe was determined that hers was not going to be one of them. That she was going to tread a different road.

Because Penny was still there in his life and had probably never been away. That was the sickening truth she somehow had to face.

'I will get over this,' she said aloud. And, more strongly, 'I will get over *him*.'

She took a drink of wine, as if toasting her own resolution, but the Sauvignon Blanc tasted oddly bitter in her throat. So she could not even rely on alcohol to numb the torment within her, she thought ruefully, putting down the glass.

Then sat bolt upright as she heard the rattle of a key in the front door. She stifled a groan. So, her aunt and uncle were back, presumably convinced she should not be left after all.

The door slammed and she heard footsteps coming hard and swift down the hall. One person. Not two. She sat up, her whole body stiffening with apprehension, her head turning towards the sitting room door as it was flung open and Darius walked in.

She said hoarsely, 'What the hell do you want?'

'I was told your so-called engagement was over and you were too heartbroken to leave the house,' he returned. He came to stand in front of her, elegant in his evening clothes, a crimson cummerbund emphasising his lean waist. His gaze swept her. 'I must say that the sackcloth and ashes are very becoming. Intriguing too,' he added softly looking at her bare feet. Chloe hastily covered them, glaring at him.

'Anyway, I decided I must come and see this phenomenon for myself,' he went on. 'Especially as I'm willing to bet good money that the disappearance of your errant swain isn't causing you even a moment's real regret, apart from a few twinges of damaged pride. So why pretend?'

'What do you know about it?' she demanded defensively, shaken equally by his sudden arrival and the awareness of her own vulnerability. The soft elderly towelling covering her was no longer a comfort but seemed to be grating against her bare skin like sandpaper.

'More than you think,' he said. 'Don't forget I've been a close observer of this curious little triangle since your return.'

'Not just an observer,' Chloe snapped back. 'You were dating Lindsay Watson yourself, after all.'

'No,' he said. 'I was not. Or not in the way you imagine. Ian had promised her months ago that he'd write to you, tell you it was over. Only he didn't, and suddenly there you were, back in town, talking about weddings. And he was still dithering. Lindsay was miserable and jealous and needed a friend.' He paused. 'Quite understandably, she wanted to make him jealous too, and as I was also involved elsewhere, I was useful.'

Involved elsewhere... The words cut into her like sharp knives. She moved restively. Changed direction.

'Just how did you manage to get in here?'

'Your Aunt Libby lent me her key.'

She gasped. 'I don't believe it. She would never do such a thing.'

He shrugged. 'All right, I lured her into the shrubbery and mugged her for it.'

She gestured impatiently. 'She really gave it to you? But why?'

'Maybe she feels she owes me,' he drawled. 'Or perhaps when I told her I was coming to collect you and whisk you to the ball like Cinderella, she decided belatedly to play Fairy Godmother. You must ask her sometime.'

'I have news for you,' said Chloe icily. 'You are not and never will be Prince Charming.'

'No hardship,' he said. 'I've always had him down as a total idiot, letting the girl he wanted run out on him because a clock struck twelve. He should have gone after her and dragged her back, rags, tatters and all.'

'Fascinating,' she said. 'Now perhaps you'd leave.'

'Not without you.' He glanced at his watch. 'So, put your dance dress on and we'll be going.'

'No,' she said fiercely. 'I won't—and we won't. I'm staying right here.'

'To perpetuate the myth of the betrayed fiancée?' He shook his head. 'That doesn't work and you know it. If you were so crazy about him, you wouldn't have gone off and left him alone for all those months. And you'd certainly have been back from time to time to stake your claim, as it were. Make him as happy as you knew how. My God, you wouldn't have been able to keep away.'

His voice slowed, became quieter. 'But that was never a problem for you, was it, Chloe? Keeping away. You must have had that poor guy climbing the walls. I wonder when it first occurred to him you weren't looking for a real man of your own, but the father you'd never known. That it wasn't intimacy or passion you were after but a safety net. While you—you couldn't see what was right under your nose. That if there'd ever been a right time with him, it had run out long ago.'

She scrambled to her feet. 'Shut up,' she said hoarsely. 'Shut up now. What the hell do you know about love or loyalty, anyway? You've never had a faithful bone in your body, so you have no right to talk to me like this. No right at all. Do you hear me?'

'And to hear is to obey?' He shook his head. 'Think again, my sweet.'

'You know nothing about it.' The words were running into each other. 'About us. Nothing. I loved Ian. I did. There was never anyone else...'

She stopped, staring at him, hearing the silence between them fill with her own ragged breathing, as she realised her denial was a nonsense born out of sheer desperation and that they both knew it.

Knew too that there was no longer anywhere for her to hide. From him or from herself.

And that she was terrified.

At last Darius said evenly, 'Shall we agree that is the last lie you will ever tell me? Now, go and change, or we'll miss the birthday toast.'

'Please—why are you making me do this?' Her voice was a pleading whisper. 'What can it matter to you whether I go or stay?'

'That,' he said, 'is something we might discuss later—when we have more time. Perhaps all the time in the world. As we should have had.'

The breath caught in her throat. She wanted to fly at him. To hit him with her fists and scream, But why didn't we? If I meant so much to you, then why did you go away with your sister-in-law? And how can you stand there—saying these things to me—reminding me of the past—when you know she's back here with you? When she's the one who's really waiting for you.

Except that she'd already gone too far down the path of self-betrayal. She could risk no more.

Instead, she lifted her chin, forcing herself to meet the intensity in his green gaze. To challenge it.

She said, 'Now who's telling lies?' Then turned, going out into the hall and up the stairs.

Darius followed.

She watched him take the key from her bedroom door and pocket it.

Cutting off what she'd hoped might be her last line of retreat.

He lifted the jade dress down from the wardrobe door and removed its protective cover.

There was a long pause, then he said softly, 'It's beautiful. And you will make it even lovelier. Put it on for me, my darling. Please.'

There was a note in his voice which, in spite of herself, turned her legs to water, and made her quiver inside.

Under her robe she was naked and they both knew it. He'd seen her without her clothes before, touched her, explored her with lingering intimacy, but that had been in some other lifetime.

My glorious, radiant girl...

Shyness paralysed her, and a sudden fear that in seven years her body might have changed. That she would not be as he remembered.

And besides, there was Penny, whom she could never allow herself to forget, no matter how deep the ache of longing to have him look at her, even touch her again. Penny, who was waiting at the ball, probably checking her wristwatch, wondering why he'd found it necessary to leave her, and how much longer she would be alone.

Penny, whom, very soon, I shall have to face, she thought.

She stared across at him mutely, her eyes enormous, begging him to understand why it had become so impossible for her to strip in front of him and heard him sigh. He put the dress carefully on the bed, then walked out of the room, closing the door behind him.

The dress had its own petticoat, so the underwear it required was minimal, just a pair of French knickers in cream satin, edged in heavy lace.

She stepped into the dress and drew it up over her body. Fastening the zip was a struggle, but she managed it in the end, because she didn't dare call him back to ask him for assistance.

Even now, she thought, and in spite of everything, I dare not trust myself.

She ranged her cosmetics on her dressing table, but decided her hands were shaking too much to do more than apply some of the clear coral lipstick that matched the polish on her toes and fingers.

It was not, she thought, a very brave face looking back at her from the mirror, but her pallor would be attributed to the fact that she'd just been jilted. No-one at the ball would expect her to be brimming with *joie de vivre.*

She hung small jade drops from her ears, collected the silver evening purse that matched her sandals, then, drawing a deep breath, she went to the door.

Darius was leaning against the wall opposite, but he straightened instantly as she appeared, his eyes raking her.

He had no right, she thought, her heartbeat quickening, to look at her with such open hunger. No right at all.

He said quietly, 'Dear God, Chloe, you take my breath away.' Then walked downstairs with her and out to the jeep in silence.

This Birthday Ball, Chloe soon realised, was a very different proposition from the last one. Last time it had seemed a pretty exclusive affair. Tonight, it appeared that everyone in the village had been invited, including Mrs Thursgood with her husband, a tall man with a heavy moustache, who was as quiet as his wife was talkative.

As Chloe walked into the ballroom, there was a sudden

hush. For a brief instant, she was sharply aware of the rustle of her taffeta skirts and the firmness of Darius's hand under her elbow, guiding her up the room, then the moment passed and everyone began chatting twice as hard.

She said in an undertone, not looking at him, 'Well, you've got me here. Perhaps you'll now permit me to join my aunt and uncle so you can enjoy the rest of your evening.'

'I'll come with you,' he said. 'After all, I have some keys to return.'

Without making a scene, there seemed little she could do. Biting her lip, she accompanied him to where the Jacksons were standing, talking to a blonde woman in pale blue.

As they approached, she turned, smiling, holding out her hand.

'Chloe,' she said. 'How lovely to see you again.'

Chloe heard her voice, small and husky, reply, 'Penny—Mrs Maynard. Good evening.'

And made herself touch the proffered fingers in a parody of goodwill.

The moment she'd dreaded had come, and it was worse than she could ever have imagined. Because the taut, thin figure she remembered was now beguilingly rounded, the proud swell of her abdomen under the gentle drape of her soft silk crepe dress proclaiming her pregnancy. The face had softened too, the happy curve of Penny's mouth suggesting that she smiled a lot these days and her eyes were shining.

She'd always been striking, but now she looked beautiful, thought Chloe with sudden anguish. Fulfilled.

Penny was turning to Darius, her glance tinged with laughing complicity. 'You're just in time, my pet. Your father's been getting restive. He wants to make the announcement.'

'Then I'd better go to him.' He paused. 'Are you feeling up to it? Because I know he wants you to come too.'

'Yes,' she said, her fingers resting briefly and protectively on her stomach. 'Of course.' Her smile swept the Jacksons, encompassing Chloe in its warmth. 'You'll excuse me for a few minutes? There'll be plenty of time to talk later while everyone's still recovering from the shock.'

Her glance rested on Chloe. 'And especially as we're going to be seeing a lot of each other in future, I hope.'

Chloe watched her go at Darius's side, her hand on his arm, then said in a low voice, 'Aunt Libby—how could you? Why did you let him do this to me? Bring me here?'

'Because I didn't really have much choice.' There was a note of tartness in the response. 'I think I've always underestimated that young man's determination to get his own way. Clearly we all have,' she added with a faint snort.

At the end of the room, Sir Gregory was being helped onto the small platform. He stood at the microphone with Darius standing on one side of him and Penny seated on the other, and Chloe could see the glances and hear the whispers, a ripple of anticipation sweeping through the room like a wind blowing across barley.

She thought, I don't want to be here. I don't want to listen to what's going to be said, and have to smile and applaud with the rest of them. I can't bear it.

But to make an exit now would attract too much attention, because the band leader was giving the signal for a short drum roll asking for silence.

Sir Gregory began slowly, leaning on his silver-topped cane. 'It is a great pleasure to see so many friends and neighbours here in this house tonight, for what will be the last ever Birthday Ball.'

He waited for the astonished murmurs to die away, then went on, 'My recent illness gave me a lot of time to reflect, on the past as well as the future. It made me see that my view of family continuity here at the Hall for the coming generations was not necessarily the right one.

'For one thing, there are increasingly difficult economic facts to be faced in maintaining a house of this size with its land.

'But, far more important, I also realised that my remaining son, now my heir, has built his own very different life elsewhere, and established business and personal commitments in Europe and other parts of the world. I cannot, in conscience, expect him to abandon any of these for another career, and other responsibilities that he never expected or desired.'

He paused. 'I have therefore decided to sell the Hall and the greater part of the estate to the Hatherstone Group to become part of their spa-hotel chain, and the deal will soon be finalised. They intend to recruit staff locally, so the sale will bring jobs to the area, and, I hope, be a whole new beginning for Willowford.'

This time, the gasp was audible.

'I have, however, retained the plantation at Warne Cross,' Sir Gregory went on. 'And will be living there in the former Keeper's Cottage, which has been refurbished and extended for me, with my good Mrs Vernon to look after me still and Mrs Denver to cook, so I expect to enjoy a very happy and stress-free existence for the time I have left. And I trust you will all come and see me from time to time.'

He added, 'Needless to say, I shall also look forward to seeing my grandchildren, when my son and the lady who is soon to be his wife bring them to visit.'

He looked slowly round the room. 'And now, I have little more to say but—goodbye and God bless you all. Oh—and on with the dance!'

'Well I'm damned,' said Uncle Hal as an excited hubbub broke out around them. 'It seems we're not the only ones downsizing, Libby, my dear.' He shook his head. 'But it certainly wasn't the announcement I expected to hear.'

'No.' His wife's tone was thoughtful, her eyes resting

shrewdly on her niece's pale face. 'But perhaps that's another deal still to be finalised.'

Chloe wasn't listening. She stood, staring ahead of her, unable to comprehend what she'd just heard. The Maynards, she thought incredulously, giving up the Hall after more than three centuries? No, it wasn't—it couldn't—be possible.

Yet that was what Sir Gregory had said, therefore it had to be believed.

So I don't have to worry about watching Darius presiding at the Hall with Penny beside him, she thought, because he has a life elsewhere, and other commitments. How ironic is that?

Or did Sir Gregory feel that installing Penny once again as lady of the manor, after all that had happened, would be just too much for the locals to accept, for all their loyalty to the Maynards?

She felt a sob rising in her throat and hastily turned it into a cough.

She said, 'It's very stuffy in here. I think I'll get some air.'

'That might be wise,' Aunt Libby said gently, and paused. 'I can see all this has come as something of a blow, darling. Did you really have no idea?'

She shook her head. 'None at all.' *Especially about Darius becoming a father...*

She forced a smile. 'But I'm sure it's all for the best.'

Because what it really means, she whispered silently, is that once I leave here, I'll never see him again. Or his wife. Or his coming baby. And 'out of sight equals out of mind'— isn't that what they say? I can only pray that it's true.

'That's right, my dear,' Uncle Hal said awkwardly. 'It's been a day of shocks altogether, but you're putting a brave face on them, and we're both proud of you. Very proud indeed. And you look a picture,' he added.

Chloe smiled again, shook her head, and made for the

French doors leading to the terrace, moving with swift determination as if she didn't see any of the people eager to detain her and talk over recent events.

And as if she hadn't noticed Darius gently helping Penny down from the platform and guiding her to the chairs at the side of the room.

With a small, bitter sigh, she went out into the darkness.

CHAPTER THIRTEEN

SHE stood for a moment, drawing deep breaths of the cool garden-scented air. Then, when she felt calmer, she walked down the steps leading down to the gardens, and descended them, carefully lifting her skirt above her ankles.

There was a stone bench just below the terrace, and she sank down onto it, listening to the wafts of music coming from the ballroom, and staring up at the starlit sky, wondering where her next view of it would come from. Not that it really mattered, she thought. All she asked was for it to be a very long way away from here. And with a lot of work to fill her days and make her too tired to stay awake at night. Or dream.

Her reverie was suddenly interrupted by the sound of footsteps on the flagstones above, and Darius's voice saying sharply, 'Chloe—where are you? I know you're out here.'

She froze incredulously, holding her breath. He'd followed her? But how was that possible—in these circumstances?

It's as if I'm being punished, she thought, goading herself into anger. But what have I done—except try and make a life for myself without him? And what blame is there in that, when he made me fall in love with him, then left me? When he's flaunting Penny in front of us all?

She waited on tenterhooks while long minutes passed, as aware of his silent presence a few yards away as if he had laid a hand on her bare shoulder. Trying hard not to shiver. Then—eventually—she heard him move away, his footsteps receding. Back to the ballroom, she thought bleakly, and to his duties as host, to his father, and to the woman carrying his child.

But she couldn't follow. Couldn't pretend any more, because she had to get away. She had money in the evening purse she was clutching like a lifeline, and there was a phone in the stables, so she could call the local taxi company and leave. Go home and pack. And tomorrow begin her next journey and find some sort of freedom.

All she had to do was cut across the gardens.

She took a deep breath then rose, shaking out her skirts, and started off across the lawn.

Only to hear his voice from behind her saying softly, triumphantly, 'At last.'

She realised in that instant that he'd gone nowhere, but simply remained where he was on the terrace, biding his time until she moved.

She tried to run but stumbled as the heel of her sandal sank into the soft turf. She wrenched herself free of it and carried on, limping clumsily and ridiculously on one bare foot.

He caught her easily within a few yards, her sandal dangling from his hand.

He said, 'When I called you Cinderella earlier, my sweet, it was meant as a joke.'

'Then perhaps I'm suffering a sense of humour failure.' She faced him defiantly, her heart hammering unevenly inside the boned confines of her bodice. 'But for me, midnight struck a long time ago, and I want to get out of here.'

'My own feelings entirely.' He sounded rueful. 'But I can't leave yet for obvious reasons, so why don't we wait a little longer and go together tomorrow?'

She was trembling almost violently. She said huskily,

'Because that isn't possible. It never was. So, please, *please* don't say things like that. Can't you show me a little mercy?'

'I already did that,' he said, slowly. 'Seven years ago when I gave you your freedom. When I began to make love to you and suddenly realised that if I took you, I would never let you go, and that you were much too young to be tied into the serious relationship that I longed for. You had your university course—your dreams of a career—your whole future waiting.'

He took a swift, harsh breath. 'I told myself that I couldn't rob you of your chance to discover who you were and what you wanted from life. That it would be cruel and unfair to ask you to give it up and come away with me, just as my mother had once warned me.

'She loved my father, but she knew how difficult it was to adjust to a life you weren't altogether ready for. And I knew I had to accept that and remove myself from temptation by going back to France the next day without you, even if it meant tearing out my heart.'

The lean face was taut, his mouth compressed.

'However, I had every intention of keeping in touch. I reasoned if I wrote to you from wherever—saw you regularly in London—that you might one day realise that what you really wanted was me. That all I had to do was wait.'

He added, 'But as we both know it didn't work out like that.'

There were tears, raw and thick in her throat. 'But you left me—for *her*.' The words she'd sworn she would never say out in the open at last.

'No,' he said steadily. 'I left *with* her. A very different situation, and forced on me when, by pure mischance, Andrew found us together in my bedroom.' He paused. 'All hell broke loose, of course. Andrew was like a crazy man, shouting accusations, calling us both every foul name he could think of, and the row brought my father down on us too.

'I knew Andrew was on the edge of violence, and my father was angrier than I'd ever seen him, and refused to listen to any kind of explanation.'

He sighed abruptly. 'I was already packed and ready to go, even before he ordered me out of the house for ever. But I felt I couldn't risk leaving Penny there alone. Therefore I took her with me to London.'

Her voice shook. 'How could you possibly explain all that—to anyone?'

'Quite easily now,' he said. He glanced around him. 'But not here. For this, we need privacy.'

Before she could stop him, he'd swept her up into his arms and carried her back across the grass to the gravel walk and round the corner of the house.

As they reached the side door and Chloe realised where she was being taken, she began to struggle.

Her voice was a gasp. 'No—I won't...'

Darius bent his head, stifling her protest swiftly and passionately with his mouth as he carried her into the house and up the stairs to his bedroom.

When, at last, he set her on her feet, she was breathless and her lips felt swollen, but she faced him stormily.

'How dare you bring me here—where you had sex with her? Where you'll no doubt spend tonight with her. Am I supposed to accept this—as if it didn't matter?'

'No,' Darius said. 'Because you're wrong on both counts. Penny and I are not and never have been lovers in this room or anywhere else. As for tonight, I imagine her husband will expect her in their bed as usual. She would have introduced him to you earlier but he was upstairs, checking on their little boy.'

There was a silence, then she said in a voice she hardly recognised as hers, 'Penny—married?'

'Very much so,' he said. 'To Jean Pierre, the friend who manages my vineyard in the Dordogne. They met a few years back when he came to London on a sales trip and were married a couple of months later.'

'But you were the one she wanted first.'

He shook his head. 'She came to me because she was desperate to leave Andrew. That was all.'

'But why—if it wasn't for you?'

Darius took her hand, leading her to the bed and sitting beside her. He said, his tone quiet, almost flat, 'Andrew and I were never particularly close, when we were children or later. He led a blameless life. I didn't. Also he was something of a loner and very conscious of being Dad's heir. He didn't seem to have many close friends, and, although he dated girls occasionally, there didn't appear to be anyone special.

'So his engagement to Penny came as something of a surprise—to me, at least. I'd no idea they were involved. But I was pleased for him. She was a stunner and fairly lively too, and I thought she might be just what he needed.

'I was away a good deal, but when I was at home I soon realised that all wasn't well between them. Andrew seemed more of an introvert than ever, and Penny was a shadow of what she'd been before the marriage. I tried once to talk to him—ask a few tactful questions—but he froze me off as usual.

'But when I came back for the Birthday Ball, I could see things had gone from bad to worse. This time I spoke to my father about it, but he glared at me and said that Andrew was a model husband, coping with a difficult and neurotic girl, and as my own private life was an open disgrace, I should kindly refrain from comment or interference.'

He took Chloe's hand, stroking her fingers gently, and the

breath caught in her throat as she responded to the promise of his skin against hers.

'What he didn't know, because I'd only just found out myself, was that my life had changed for ever, dating from the moment I went to the Willow Pond for a swim and found a dark-haired siren sitting on a rock, waiting for me to fall in love with her.'

She bent her head, letting her hair fall around her flushed face, the turmoil within her changing to a different kind of excitement.

'Because fall I did,' he went on. 'Between one breath and the next.' He gave an unsteady laugh. 'I'd never been so happy, knowing for the first time I had someone to work for—to plan a future beside. But I couldn't ignore what was going on around me, especially when Penny started seeking me out, telling me she needed to talk.

'I was pretty sure Andrew had noticed this too, so I was careful to keep my distance, which, in retrospect, was a mistake, because I failed to realise how near the edge she really was.

'The ball finished earlier than usual that year, and I was thankful, because I'd found having to go on being civil was almost impossible when I was feeling so raw over you. When I came up here, I could still smell your perfume on my pillow, remember how glorious you'd looked, and how your eyes had smiled into mine.'

He took a sharp breath. 'I told myself that I'd been a fool to let you go. That it wasn't too late to drive over to the Grange and say, "I will love you for the rest of my life. Come away with me now and we'll be married as soon as I can get a licence".'

'You wanted to tell me that?' Her voice shook. 'Oh, why didn't you?'

'For all the excellent reasons already stated,' Darius said

ruefully. 'Plus I was terrified you might say no. It seemed best to stick to my plan for a lengthy and patient wooing.'

He sighed. 'Just as well I didn't know exactly how long, or that when we met again you'd claim to love someone else. I fell asleep that night thinking about you, wanting you, and when someone touched my shoulder and said my name, I suppose I hoped it was you. That by some miracle you'd come back to me and our life together could begin.'

He paused. 'Instead, I found Penny standing by my bed in her dressing gown. She said, "When you leave tomorrow, you have to take me with you. I can't bear any more. My cousin Helen in Kensington will let me stay there until I sort myself out. I'm just going to take my clothes—not my car or anything else Andrew has given me. That wouldn't be right".'

'I thought at first she'd been drinking, and wondered how I could get her back to her own room when the house was still full of people clearing up after the ball. But I couldn't get out of bed either, because I always sleep naked, so I was stuck both ways.

'I tried to sound soothing—said I was sure it couldn't be as bad as all that, and suggested she got Andrew to take her away somewhere romantic on a second honeymoon.'

He grimaced. 'And with that the floodgates opened. She collapsed on the bed beside me, crying her eyes out. Told me it had never been a real marriage. That Andrew had made a few half-hearted attempts to have sex with her in the first couple of weeks, but they'd ended in failure, and they no longer even shared a room. She claimed he'd never loved her, and had married her only for an heir to the Maynard name, except he couldn't force himself to do what was necessary. And my father had begun dropping pointed hints.'

'Oh, God.' Chloe drew a shaken breath. 'How awful for her. For them both.'

'But she hadn't finished,' Darius said grimly. 'And this

was the worst of all. She said maybe Andrew wasn't the kind of man who should be married, or not to a woman anyway. Except that was something he wouldn't admit, even to himself.

'And while I was still reeling from that, the door opened and Andrew himself came in with my father close behind him, and found her on the bed with my arm round her.'

He shuddered. 'God, it was terrible. He was shouting he'd always suspected there was something going on. Accused us of meeting secretly in London. Said she was nothing but a dirty tart.'

Chloe gasped. 'But he couldn't have meant it.'

'Not unless he saw it as a convenient way of getting rid of a girl who'd become an embarrassment—a living reproach in his own home. And apart from the obvious denials there wasn't much we could say. Penny wasn't prepared to tax Andrew with his failings as a husband in front of his father, and I respected her for that.'

She said quietly, 'Poor Penny, knowing her life was in pieces and unable to do anything about it.' She hesitated. 'But should you be telling me all this? Won't she hate my knowing these things?'

'It was her own idea. She's always felt that, by asking my help, she cost me my family, my home and the girl I loved for seven whole years. She told me she needed to set the record straight.'

She said, 'Did she tell your father—about the marriage?'

'She didn't have to.' Darius sighed again. 'Andrew wrote to him before that last climbing trip, saying he'd realised the truth about himself a long time ago, but had never been able to accept it. Saw it as some kind of betrayal of his heritage. I think the rogue horses and dangerous sports were just symbols of the ongoing struggle his life became.'

He shook his head. 'It was the letter combined with the

shock of his death that probably triggered Dad's stroke. On the other hand, while he was recovering, it changed his perceptions of a great many things, as he made clear tonight. But, I believed it was much too late for me. Because, when I tried to contact you afterwards and explain, your aunt sent me away, saying you were totally disgusted and never wanted to see me or speak to me again.'

His mouth twisted. 'I'd been condemned without a word in my own defence and that hurt, so I left bitter and angry.'

He added softly, 'But I couldn't forget you, Chloe, no matter how hard I tried. Then I heard you were coming back, and I felt I'd been offered another chance.'

She began to smile. 'You weren't very nice to me when we met that first time.'

His mouth relaxed into a teasing grin. 'You thought I was someone else. And then you hit me with your supposed engagement. I knew Lindsay and Ian were an item and I thought you were simply using him as an excuse to keep me at bay.'

She said in a low voice, 'I think I was. I told myself I couldn't bear to be hurt again. So I tried to fight my feelings and lost every time. I only wanted to stay away tonight because I'd heard Penny was back. When I saw she was pregnant, I thought it must be your baby, and that you were going to marry her and the pain of that was so bad I had to run away.'

He said gently, 'My darling, there's only one girl in the world I've ever wanted to be my wife and the mother of my children.' He paused. 'I said earlier, I was prepared for a long and patient wooing, but my patience has almost run out.' He smoothed back her hair, cupping the curve of her face in his hand as he looked into her eyes. 'I want you so much, my sweet one. Are you still going to make me wait?'

Her whole body clenched in sweet, fierce yearning. She

moved into his arms, her hands gripping his shoulders through the layers of cloth, her lips already parting for his kiss.

His mouth was warm and urgent on hers, his hands trembling as he dealt with the long zip at the back of her dress, peeling the jade taffeta away from her body, and dropping it to the floor.

She clung to him, gasping as his crisp dress shirt grazed her bared breasts, her hands stroking his hair, offering him kiss for kiss in the rising tumult of their mutual desire, so long unsatisfied.

His hands caressed her body, moving over her skin in something like wonderment as if he still could not believe that she was here with him—about to be his at last.

His lips traversed the supple line of her throat, letting his tongue make a delicate foray into the inner whorls of her ear, his teeth nibbling delicately at its lobe, while his hands moved down to cup her breasts in his palms and tease each rosy nipple into aching arousal with his fingertips.

She murmured his name pleadingly, her own mouth tracing the strong line of his neck.

When he released her it was only to tug back the covers on the bed, and place her gently against the pillows. He began to strip off his own clothes, his eyes scanning restlessly down her body, still partly concealed by her silk-and-lace knickers.

He said quietly and huskily, 'Take them off.'

She obeyed, wriggling out of them slowly, languorously, smiling up at him as she watched his emerald gaze kindle. He was naked too, now, and she held out her arms to receive him.

They came together in a breathless, almost anguished silence. Chloe had only instinct and her own burning need to guide her as she held him, opened herself to him. As she found herself welcoming the swift lancing pain of his first penetration of her because it meant she belonged to him completely at last. To him and to no-one else—ever.

And as she lifted her hips to meet each long, heated thrust of total possession, locking her slim legs round his waist to draw him into her ever more deeply, wanting to please him—to satisfy him—to make him forget every other woman he'd ever held in his arms.

Only to discover how richly her generosity was to be rewarded, as the driving force of his lean body ignited new and undreamed of sensations in her inexperienced flesh.

Darius changed his position slightly, so that his hardness came into sensuous contact with her tiny hidden mound, deliberately and deliciously arousing its exquisite sensitivity. Taking her to some edge and beyond.

Chloe could feel the first ripples of pleasure in her innermost self. Recognised with bewilderment the moment when they began to build into a mindless spiral of delight. Tried for an instant to resist their mounting intensity, scared by her own response, only to find herself overtaken, overwhelmed by a harsh, scalding ecstasy that had her sobbing with incoherent joy into his mouth.

And heard his own almost agonised cry of rapture echo hers.

Afterwards he held her wrapped in his arms, his lips against her hair, whispering words she had never heard before. Never believed she would hear.

She lay, her head pillowed on his shoulder, and knew that all the safety and security she had ever wanted was here with her now, and always would be.

Eventually, he said lazily, 'At some point, we're going to have to dress and go downstairs. It's the last Birthday Ball, and I need to dance with you.'

'Oh.' Chloe stirred guiltily. 'What will people think?'

'The truth probably, but what do we care? We won't be here when the rumour mill starts.'

'We won't?'

He shook his head. 'I have to go back to France tomorrow. The vineyard needs my attention.' He paused. 'But it occurs to me that this may not be what you want, or not on a permanent basis. The deal with Hatherstone hasn't gone through yet, and I know how much Willowford has always meant to you. So if you want to live here—have the Hall, the title, the whole bit—it can still be done. The choice is entirely yours.'

'None of those things mean anything to me,' she said, adding simply, 'I never thought of them as mine, anyway.'

'Ah,' he said, and she heard the smile in his voice. 'So if I say to you, my adorable angel, "Come with me now, and we'll be married as soon as I can get a licence", what will you reply?'

'What I'd have said seven years ago if you'd asked me.' Chloe turned her head, pressing her lips to the pulse in his throat. 'That my life is yours, wherever it takes us, now and for ever.'

Darius said softly, 'I think you just rewrote the marriage service.' And began to kiss her again.

* * * * *

CLASSIC

You can find more information on upcoming Harlequin®
titles, free excerpts and more at www.Harlequin.com.

HPCNM0312

REQUEST YOUR
FREE BOOKS!

2 FREE NOVELS PLUS
2 FREE GIFTS!

YES! Please send me 2 FREE Harlequin Presents® novels and my 2 FREE gifts (gifts are worth about $10). After receiving them, if I don't wish to receive any more books, I can return the shipping statement marked "cancel." If I don't cancel, I will receive 6 brand-new novels every month and be billed just $4.30 per book in the U.S. or $4.99 per book in Canada. That's a saving of at least 14% off the cover price! It's quite a bargain! Shipping and handling is just 50¢ per book in the U.S. and 75¢ per book in Canada.* I understand that accepting the 2 free books and gifts places me under no obligation to buy anything. I can always return a shipment and cancel at any time. Even if I never buy another book, the two free books and gifts are mine to keep forever.

106/306 HDN FERQ

Name _____ (PLEASE PRINT)

Address _____ Apt. #

City _____ State/Prov. _____ Zip/Postal Code

Signature (if under 18, a parent or guardian must sign)

Mail to the **Reader Service:**
IN U.S.A.: P.O. Box 1867, Buffalo, NY 14240-1867
IN CANADA: P.O. Box 609, Fort Erie, Ontario L2A 5X3

Not valid for current subscribers to Harlequin Presents books.

Are you a current subscriber to Harlequin Presents books and want to receive the larger-print edition?
Call 1-800-873-8635 or visit www.ReaderService.com.

* Terms and prices subject to change without notice. Prices do not include applicable taxes. Sales tax applicable in N.Y. Canadian residents will be charged applicable taxes. Offer not valid in Quebec. This offer is limited to one order per household. All orders subject to credit approval. Credit or debit balances in a customer's account(s) may be offset by any other outstanding balance owed by or to the customer. Please allow 4 to 6 weeks for delivery. Offer available while quantities last.

Your Privacy—The Reader Service is committed to protecting your privacy. Our Privacy Policy is available online at www.ReaderService.com or upon request from the Reader Service.

We make a portion of our mailing list available to reputable third parties that offer products we believe may interest you. If you prefer that we not exchange your name with third parties, or if you wish to clarify or modify your communication preferences, please visit us at www.ReaderService.com/consumerschoice or write to us at Reader Service Preference Service, P.O. Box 9062, Buffalo, NY 14269. Include your complete name and address.

Harlequin *Romance*

Get swept away with a brand-new miniseries by USA TODAY *bestselling author*

MARGARET WAY

The Langdon Dynasty

Amelia Norton knows that in order to embrace her future, she must first face her past. As she unravels her family's secrets, she is forced to turn to gorgeous cattleman Dev Langdon for support—the man she vowed never to fall for again.

Against the haze of the sweltering Australian heat Mel's guarded exterior begins to crumble...and Dev will do whatever it takes to convince his childhood sweetheart to be his bride.

THE CATTLE KING'S BRIDE
Available April 2012

And look for
ARGENTINIAN IN THE OUTBACK
Coming in May 2012

Taft Bowman knew he'd ruined any chance he'd had for happiness with Laura Pendleton when he drove her away years ago...and into the arms of another man, thousands of miles away. Now she was back, a widow with two small children...and despite himself, he was starting to believe in second chances.

Harlequin Special® Edition® presents a new installment in USA TODAY *bestselling author RaeAnne Thayne's miniseries,* THE COWBOYS OF COLD CREEK.

Enjoy a sneak peek of A COLD CREEK REUNION

Available April 2012 from Harlequin® Special Edition®

A younger woman stood there, and from this distance he had only a strange impression, as though she was somehow standing on an island of calm amid the chaos of the scene, the flashing lights of the emergency vehicles, shouts between his crew members, the excited buzz of the crowd.

And then the woman turned and he just about tripped over a snaking fire hose somebody shouldn't have left there.

Laura.

He froze, and for the first time in fifteen years as a firefighter, he forgot about the incident, his mission, just what the hell he was doing here.

Laura.

Ten years. He hadn't seen her in all that time, since the week before their wedding when she had given him back his ring and left town. Not just town. She had left the whole damn country, as if she couldn't run far enough to get away from him.

Some part of him desperately wanted to think he had made some kind of mistake. It couldn't be her. That was just some other slender woman with a long sweep of honey-blond hair and big, blue, unforgettable eyes. But no. It was definitely Laura. Sweet and lovely.

Not his.

He was going to have to go over there and talk to her. He didn't want to. He wanted to stand there and pretend he hadn't seen her. But he was the fire chief. He couldn't hide out just because he had a painful history with the daughter of the property owner.

Sometimes he hated his job.

Will Taft and Laura be able to make the years recede...or is the gulf between them too broad to ever cross?

Find out in
A COLD CREEK REUNION
Available April 2012 from Harlequin® Special Edition®
wherever books are sold.

Celebrate the 30th anniversary
of Harlequin® Special Edition® with a bonus story
included in each Special Edition® book in April!

HSEEXP0412

ROMANTIC
SUSPENSE

Danger is hot on their heels!

Catch the thrill with author

LINDA CONRAD

Chance, Texas

Sam Chance, a U.S. marshal in the Witness Security
Service, is sworn to protect Grace Brown and her
one-year-old son after Grace testifies against an infamous
drug lord and he swears revenge. With Grace on the edge of
fleeing, Sam knows there is only one safe place he can take
her—home. But when the danger draws near, it's not just
Sam's life on the line but his heart, too.

Watch out for

Texas Baby Sanctuary

Available April 2012

Texas Manhunt

Available May 2012

www.Harlequin.com

HRS27772

red-hot reads

Sizzling fairy tales
to make every fantasy come true!

Fan-favorite authors
Tori Carrington and Kate Hoffmann
bring readers

Blazing Bedtime Stories, Volume VI

MAID FOR HIM...

Successful businessman Kieran Morrison doesn't dare hope for
a big catch when he goes fishing. But when he wakes up one
night to find a beautiful woman seemingly unconscious on the
deck of his sailboat, he lands one bigger than he could ever
have imagined by way of mermaid Daphne Moore.
But is she real? Or just a fantasy?

OFF THE BEATEN PATH

Greta Adler and Alex Hansen have been friends for seven years.
So when Greta agrees to accompany Alex at a mountain retreat
owned by a client, she doesn't realize that Alex has a different
path he wants their relationshiop to take.
But will Greta follow his lead?

Available April 2012 wherever books are sold.

www.Harlequin.com

HB79679